ROSE TREMAIN

The author, who was chosen as one of the Best of Young British Novelists in 1983, has had five novels published: SADLER'S BIRTHDAY, LETTER TO SISTER BENEDICTA, THE CUPBOARD, THE SWIMMING POOL SEASON and RESTORATION. The latter won the Sunday Express Book of the Year Award in 1989, was short-listed for the Booker Prize and won the Angel Literary Award, as did THE SWIMMING POOL SEASON in 1985. She has also written two volumes of short stories: THE COLONEL'S DAUGHTER AND OTHER STORIES, which won the Dylan Thomas Prize, and THE GARDEN OF THE VILLA MOLLINI. She has had performed numerous plays on television and radio including the award-winning TEMPORARY SHELTER. She teaches creative writing at the University of East Anglia and reviews regularly for the radio and press.

Rose Tremain

SADLER'S BIRTHDAY

First published in Great Britain in this edition in hardback in 1989 by Hamish Hamilton Ltd.

Sceptre edition, 1990

Sceptre is an imprint of Hodder and Stoughton Paperbacks, a division of Hodder and Stoughton Ltd.

A CIP catalogue record for this book is available from the British Library.

ISBN 0-340-51604-6

Printed and bound in Great Britain for Hodder and Stoughton Paperbacks, a division of Hodder and Stoughton Ltd., Mill Road, Dunton Green, Sevenoaks, Kent TN13 2YA. (Editorial Office: 47 Bedford Square, London WC1B 3DP) by Richard Clay Ltd., Bungay, Suffolk.

For Jon

SADLER'S BIRTHDAY

I

Jack Sadler woke up in what had once been the Colonel's room. Now, like the rest of the big house, it was his. They'd had a wing each, the Colonel and his wife Madge; they liked to meet at mealtimes in the dining room, listen to the news together, or play a game of Gin Rummy, but several doors divided them while they slept.

Colonel Bassett had been a tidy man. Came from his army training, so he said. Never so much as a hair out of place on him except, as he got older, in his ears where they sprouted untended. It was always a mystery to Sadler why so meticulous a man had allowed this one part of himself to become so very overgrown.

Sadler looked round the room. The Colonel had been very fond of cupboards. He had put them in all over the house, so that whenever he saw something lying around, he could be sure to be near one and just pop it away out of sight. At least once a year he'd turned out all the cupboards and made inventories of what they held.

It was cold in the room, so cold that Sadler lay there without moving, wrapped in his blankets and his two eiderdowns, lay trapped by the morning cold, cursing himself for not leaving the fire on all night. He thought to himself, never minded an East Anglian winter when I was a lad. Quite enjoyed an excuse to wear my green balaclava. But now. He was seventy-six, give or take a day or two (he knew his birthday was coming round soon, one day this week or next – he'd have to look at the calendar) and the cold seemed to wake up all the little aches and pains that dozed in his joints, even set the bile in his stomach trickling backwards into his throat.

Don't get up, he thought. Don't move. Lie here all day in the warm bed. Just clamber out for a second or two, long enough to turn on the fire, then back into the warm. Lie there, arms straight down, waiting for the fire to come red. Wait till the room's nice and warm, then prop yourself up with another pillow, put your dressing gown on and your glasses and have a little read . . .

He lay rigid. Cowardly old sod, he thought. Get the bleedin' fire on or you'll be trapped like this all day. So silly when it wouldn't take more than a few seconds, just the time it takes to walk four and a half paces.

Then he remembered the dog. He looked at his clock, saw half past seven and knew that by now the dog would be scratching at the kitchen door, desperate for a pee but so well trained poor old thing he only did it on the floor if he had to. Sadler never had known what kind of dog he was: brown wiry body, black eyes and no tail to speak of, just a small woolly tuft to wag. From behind he looked like a little brown sheep. One hundred and five he was by human computing and except at moments like this Sadler was glad of his company. He often wondered what it would be like to be totally alone with not so much as a yap to break the silence and no one to read the paper to. He sincerely hoped he would die before the dog, recognizing at the same time that this thought was a bit Colonelish. Because the Colonel always used to say, 'You know, Sadler, the only thing that's bearable about death is that I'll die first, before Madge.' And then in the end Madge and the Colonel had died on the same day, Coronation Day.

Sadler sat up in bed and fumbled about for his dressing gown. At the window, heavy chintz curtains held out the sunlight. March morning, cold as January, but clear as a jewel in the grounds of the great house. Sadler switched on the fire, resisted the impulse that drove him back to bed, went to the window instead, big south window where the merest twitching of the curtains sent sunlight jumping over the sill.

Everything he could see from this window belonged to him: a wide lawn, cut in two by the drive and sweeping leftwards past the house, right round to the north side. Beyond the lawn, an old yew hedge like a line of sentinel shoulders hunched at the gate of a wood of evergreens. To the right of the lawn, the apple orchard, walled on one side but straggling over rising ground to a meadow. At the bottom of the meadow, a stream tunnelling a windy course among dense rushes, never flowing fast enough to stay clear but in late spring its banks gaudy with kingcups. This morning everything was white with frost. Much prettier than snow, Sadler always thought, much more delicate. But spring was such a fickle whore. Daffs couldn't push up innocent shiny buds without she sent a frost to snap them off.

The dog was whining now, would be crossing his little legs if he could. Sadler heard the whining as he came barefoot down the wide stairs and thought, time I took him to the vet again to see about his worm. He seems happy with his worm, though. Fond of being hungry all the time, makes him feel young again I wouldn't wonder. Funny things, worms. Worm lies trapped in his belly, eating for him, eating and growing fat and the dog's as thin as a fox.

It was too late when Sadler opened the kitchen door. The dog sat silent, reproachful, looking at the puddle he'd made. Sadler never scolded the dog, couldn't bear to do it any more. He patted the dog's little head, opened the door to the garden and sent him trotting out into the cold. Five minutes and he'd be whining again, asking to be let in.

Sadler sat down at the kitchen table, wondering how many countless mornings had there been, just like this one, sitting there thinking to himself, twenty years ago I'd be up and dressed by now, smart enough in my morning uniform – black trousers, striped cotton jacket, clean white shirt and one of the Colonel's old ties – chivvying Vera who moved so ponderously about the kitchen, watching the clock to be sure to sound the gong on the dot of eight. Then waiting there, standing almost to attention, for the Colonel to come down at one minute past.

'Good morning, Sadler.'

'Good morning, Sir.'

Handing him *The Times* as he went into the dining room, following him in, serving his eggs or his kidneys or his sausages, pouring his strong coffee and then retiring with a nod and a 'thank you, Sadler'. Back to the kitchen then, watching Vera's thin hands decorating the butter balls with a sprig of parsley, putting the finishing touches to Madam's tray. What a neat little breakfast she took every day: lightly boiled egg, lightly toasted bread, a little pot of china tea and a slice of lemon.

'Ready, Vera?'

'Yes, Mr Sadler.'

Lifting the tray up with pride, it looked so nice with its clean linen traycloth (Madam always bought her tray-cloths from the Ladies Work Stall at the Hentswell fête, they were so finely embroidered), carrying it up the wide staircase to her room. And there she was, sitting up in bed in her bed-jacket, her rouge on already, smiling at him.

'Good morning, Sadler.'

'Good morning, Madam.'

Still smiling. 'Is the Colonel down?'

'I've just served his breakfast, Madam.'

No one to carry a tray to any more. Dead and gone now, the smiling face. And he'd never known it when it was young and pretty. Lined and rouged already when he had taken up service under its kindly eye. Older than the Colonel, his Madge. Twenty-six she'd been as the century

4

turned and she'd gone on her father's arm to St Margaret's Westminster. And her groom only twenty, not long out of school, a young lieutenant with hardly the need to shave more than twice a week. What a wedding! A thousand lilies at the altar alone. Friends of royalty in the congregation, quite a crowd in Parliament Square to see the bride and groom come out. Madge remembered her wedding day all her life, just as if it had been yesterday. She told Sadler that her mother had spent *forty-three shillings a yard* on ivory satin for her dress and when she'd put it on and her maid had handed her the bouquet she'd felt as good as a queen.

The dog was scratching at the door.

'Come on then,' Sadler called, 'never seen a door before?'

He chuckled, got up slowly and shuffled over the stone floor to let the dog in. It went at once to its warm mat by the old Aga, lay down and look up at Sadler who remembered the puddle and cursed.

'Incontinent little rat!'

The dog wagged its clump of a tail, might have smiled if it could have.

'Come on then, sod you,' Sadler said, 'better mop it up.'

He found an old cloth under the sink, ran a cold tap on to it and wrung it out. His back hurt as he bent down to wipe the floor. What a dose of humiliation old age could give you. What a creaking, stinking, barnacled old wreck life made of the boat in which your soul was forced to sail. Might live another twenty years in this ghastly old body, Sadler thought as he pushed the cloth to and fro. 'But all I can say, God, if you're there,' he said aloud, 'is I hope not.' He straightened up painfully, went back to the sink and rinsed out the cloth. Then he crossed to the Aga and the dog looked up.

'If you think you're going to get a meal, you're wrong, friend,' he said. He would have patted the dog, to give it reassurance that he cared about it, but he couldn't bear the thought of bending down again. 'Later,' he said, touching the dog with his foot, 'just make myself a cup of tea and then I'll get you something. You be a good boy.'

Sadler had come to the house as the Second World War began. He was thirty-nine then and fit as any who boarded the troop ships for France, but he limped just a little as he had done from birth, enough, they said, not to have to fight. Late in September he came down to London from a job in Scarborough, spent a day or two in a boarding house in the Charing Cross Road and then caught a train for Norwich.

He was met by the Colonel's chauffeur in the Austin Seven. Cold autumn day in 1939. A winter wind blowing through Norfolk, straight from Russia.

'You must be Mr Sadler.'

'Yes indeed. Cold isn't it?'

'Very cold, Mr Sadler. My name's Wren, Sir, the Colonel's chauffeur.'

Smart little cap, nice kid gloves and a lovely shine on his worn boots, Wren sat bolt upright at the wheel, driving as carefully as he dressed. Must be sixty-five, Sadler thought, sitting beside him. More at home with a pony and trap probably than with the Austin. Less than ten miles to do and it took them best part of an hour.

'She's a good little car,' Wren said as they set out, 'but she don't go.'

Sadler pondered this saying for most of the journey, sitting silent, smiling to himself, looking out at the wide fields. Wren, intent on the road, liable to slow almost to a halt each time a car came the other way, only spoke a couple more times. Once he said 'Did you have a good train journey, Mr Sadler?' and Sadler, who liked trains, replied 'Oh most enjoyable, thank you.' Then, as they

6

neared the house, Wren took a nervous hand off the wheel to point ahead to the gates.

'There you are, Mr Sadler. The house of course is hidden from the road.'

They swept into the drive, Wren full of daring now that they were off the public road. Sadler put his hat on, thought nervously that it wouldn't be long till dinner-time and of course Madam would expect him to serve. There might even be guests and who knew in what state of preparedness he would find the kitchen staff.

Leaves flew like a flock of golden sparrows as they drove down an avenue of beech, and then there at last was the house, perfect copy, so the history books ran, of one of Queen Victoria's favourite residences, yellowish in its stone skin with a gleam of sun on it.

'Well,' said Wren, 'there she is.'

The house he meant, did he? Or was it Mrs Bassett with a nice smile on her lips coming out of the porch? There she stood watching them as Wren brought the car to a stop, got out quickly and stood to attention. Sadler fumbled with his door handle, wished he'd paid the landlady in Charing Cross to press his suit, stepped out on to the gravel and into the orbit of the smile.

'Sadler.'

'How d'you do, Madam.'

'Did you have a pleasant journey?'

'Most enjoyable, thank you.'

'You're not too tired, then?'

'Oh no.'

A voice from within. 'Did I hear the car, Madge?'

And then the Colonel materialized, shoved a wide red hand into Sadler's and smiled the smile that had earned him a reputation for frankness in the regiment, the smile that had stiffened and narrowed just a little since the day, forty years before, when it had lighted Madge's wedding.

They guided him in, leaving his suitcase in the car and

7

Wren, still stiff and straight like a bowling pin in the middle of the drive. Into the lofty hall, the meeting point for numerous doors and passageways. To the right, Sadler glimpsed a comfortable, heavily curtained room where a coal fire burned, the shut door on the left he guessed would be the dining room. But on of course, away from the splendour, leaving the Colonel behind, to the furthest passageway, cold as they entered it, that led to the kitchen and the servants' hall.

Sadler heard a chatter of voices – Vera and her kitchen maids like a scrawny chicken and her brood of two. But as Sadler and Madge entered they stopped all movement and Sadler found that he was looking at three apprehensive faces. He smiled and heard Madam say 'This is Mr Sadler', held out his hand to the cook who wiped hers on her apron and shook his limply. The kitchen maids bobbed and Sadler felt a blush coming to his face, remembered bitterly how his mother always had her curtsey ready for Milady, used to practise it in front of her looking glass . . .

'My cook, Mrs Prinz, who likes us to call her Vera, and this is Jane and Betty who help her in the kitchen.'

His army. This thin, tired woman with her pert helpers.

'Pleased to meet you,' said Vera.

'You must be tired.' From Madam.

'Oh no.'

'Come and see your room and then I expect you'd like to unpack.'

Sadler remembered his suitcase.

'Thank you.'

He followed Mrs Bassett back down the cold passage, through a door and up a flight of stairs, green linoleum on them. Out on to a landing, carpeted with coconut matting, then past her while she stood at another door, holding it open for him, into such a nice little room, not large by any standards but wonderfully neat.

8

'Do you think you'll have enough room for your things?'

'Oh yes.'

'You'll find a rug in the wardrobe if there's not enough blankets on your bed.'

'The nights are getting cold in this part, I wouldn't wonder.'

'I'm afraid so. It's been such a wonderful summer, but it's over now.'

Sadler was caught by the measure of despair in her voice, looked at her and thought: how will war touch us here? And into his head came this odd picture of the chauffeur falling down where he stood so smartly to attention, knocked down like a skittle and his body rolling away under the car.

'Wren will bring up your suitcase.'

'Thank you, Madam.'

'We dine at eight fifteen.'

'Very good.'

'You may wear a short coat to serve in the dining room, except when we entertain.'

And then she was gone, leaving him to his room. He looked all round it, noting the simplicity of the things in it and finding them pleasing. Then he saw the picture above his bed, a gentle pastoral scene, belonging more correctly in a nursery – two fat little children, boy and girl, picking daisies in some wonderland of a meadow. Sparrows and thrushes, fat too and friendly, hopping about near them and in the distance an old water wheel. Sadler laughed. The room reminded him of a room he'd shared with his mother countless years back, the year they'd gone to Milady's house. Put to bed at six without much in the way of supper, he'd lie straight as a stick waiting for his mother to finish work and get into bed beside him. She was usually there by eight for she'd be up again before dawn. He remembered how when she climbed into bed he'd turn towards her, pretending to roll over in his sleep, and feel

9

the warmth and smell of her body soothing him. There'd been a child's picture in that room too. His mother had said Milady had put it there especially for him. But he didn't believe that and one evening, before his mother came up, he took it off the wall to see if there was a pale patch on the wall behind it and there was. There was even dust on the wire.

Sadler got up and closed the window. It looked out over the orchard, untidy with fallen fruit, its leaves reddish and impatient to be gone. So quiet it was up there in this room. Impossible to think of war in that silence. He took his jacket off and hung it up.

Dining alone, the Colonel and his Madge sat either end of the mahogany table and Sadler, smart in his short black jacket, trod the distances in between. His practised hand served them with an ease and elegance which, on that first evening, gave Madge the satisfaction of knowing she had 'found her man'. Unobtrusive in a corner of the long room, Sadler waited absolutely silent and still while they ate, politely deaf, politely invisible.

'Did you catch the news at six, dear?'

'Barricades they're talking about now.'

'What sort of barricades?'

'Well, roadblocks on all routes into London from the coast.'

'Really? That'll be terribly inconvenient, surely.'

'Yes. And it'll be our lot, us Local Defence chappies, who'll have all the work.'

'Anything else?'

'On the news?'

'Yes.'

'Nothing much. No one seems to be able to make their minds up about rationing.'

'Well I wish they would. Its very difficult not knowing where we stand.'

'Bound to come sooner or later.'

'I thought it was the Germans that were meant to be having food shortages.'

'Depends on the blockade, Madge. What no one seems to realize is that Italy is quite unreliable.'

'What about the children? Nothing about that? I can't believe they won't give us a decent warning.'

'What children?'

'On the nine o'clock news last night they said they were preparing to send thousands more out of London. I mean, if people are going to be asked to open their homes to strangers I would have thought it only fair that they should be able to choose whom they get.'

'May not happen, dear.'

'It's happening, Geoffrey. They've sent hundreds out already – *millions* I believe.'

'Well, no one's asked us to take any.'

'It's probably just a question of time.'

Sadler listened to their talk of the war. It was, he thought, as if an earthquake somewhere else was sending almost imperceptible shudders across their shoulders. And the Colonel, well, he'd do his bit for the Home Guard, but he had to admit that he was glad to be safe at home with Madge and he knew, not without shame, that the part of him that had wanted to die for England had died.

They ambled out of the dining room, asked Sadler to bring their coffee to them by the drawing room fire and gave him a smile as they left, relieved at last to have found a butler who seemed so unobtrusive and careful, and quite determined to treat him well.

His first evening's duties complete, Sadler went to the servants' hall, a long awkward room with a square of carpet in the middle of the floor, a couple of old sofas and a table and four chairs by the window. Vera, half asleep with her knitting on her knee, would have scrambled to her feet when he came in.

'Lord no, Mrs Prinz,' he said, 'there's no need for that.

I've no doubt at all you've earned the rest.'

She smiled at him, a nervous doubting smile, and said: 'Don't know what's the matter with me these days; sit down for a couple of minutes and find I'm nodding off.'

'You have a long day.'

'No more'n it always were. Course, that's not a complaint when I say that. I wouldn't want you thinking I'd any complaints, for I'm not one for grumbling – only about m'self. You could say it was a complaint againt m'self.'

Sadler sat down, glad to be off his feet. Whenever he found himself with strangers he tooks pains to disguise his limp as much as he could and the effort always made his legs ache. Vera took up her knitting.

'Of course,' she said after a while, 'things 'aven't been right 'ere.'

Sadler was cautious. 'No?'

'I was on the point of leaving. I'd even told Madam, because I couldn't live in the same house with 'im, Mr Sadler. I had to go and tell her "I can't work with that man any more".'

'Who would that be?'

'Mr Goss. It was a wonder Madam didn't lose all 'er staff. The way he treated some of us.'

'The butler?'

'Not good at his job either, you know. Such a big man. Got in the way all the time.'

'Happy to see him leave, were you then?'

'I'd say. I told Madam, it was either me or 'im.'

'What was it that he did, Mrs Prinz?'

'Vera – I do prefer Vera.' She put down her knitting and leant forward on her chair. 'There was something evil about that man. He liked to see a person suffer.'

'That's not right, is it.'

'Just loved to pass a personal remark, make you feel awkward.'

She went on in a whisper: 'He sat down on that settee one evening, right where you're sittin' now, Mr Sadler, and he turned to me and said: "Prinz – now that'd be a German name, wouldn't it?" I mean you can't call that kind, can you? In time of war. Of course I didn't answer 'im. I just got right up and walked out of the room. Betty was here. She told me afterwards he'd looked quite surprised when I went out, had the cheek to ask her what he'd done wrong. But it was all over for me then. I couldn't go on working with a man like that. And they value me 'ere, Mr Sadler, the Colonel and Madam, they know what I'm worth, they know I'm loyal. In fact the Colonel was quite upset when he heard about the trouble. He sent for me and said: "I can't be doing with that kind of unpleasantness in the servants' hall." "There's enough trouble in the world," he said, "without bringing any into my own house." Of course, I personally think they'd never taken to Goss. As I say, 'e wasn't a good servant – too cocksure of 'imself and too clumsy. I used to wonder 'e could get between the chairs in the dining room, he had such a girth on 'im.'

'Where was he from, Mrs Prinz?'

'Vera, Mr Sadler. I do prefer it.'

'Oh Vera, yes.'

'Yorkshire, so he said, but I said to Betty "that doesn't sound like Yorkshire to me" and we never did find out.'

'My last position was in Yorkshire.'

'Oh yes, Mr Sadler?'

'In Scarborough.'

'On the coast then?'

'Oh yes, quite near the sea.'

'I used to like a nice swim. I'm from London – you can tell that can't you? But my mum always took me to the seaside come August. Too 'ot to breathe in town, she used to say, and off we'd go, me and 'er on the train.'

'And your husband, did he like the sea?'

'Oh no.'

Then she went quiet, picked up her knitting, middle of a row, and set the needles clacking. Whenever Vera knitted, her jaw dropped and her mouth came open. Sadler felt pity for her, with her thin body and her anxious face and her pride.

It wasn't much after nine by the clock on the mantlepiece, but Sadler found himself yawning, thinking longingly of his neat quiet room. He stood up.

'I'll be turning in then, Vera.'

'Oh yes.' She kept her eyes fastened on her knitting.

'Good night then.'

'Good night, Mr Sadler.'

He shut the door behind him, came out into the cold passage and then climbed the green lino stairs. On the coconut matting landing he paused, letting himself enjoy the last few paces that took him to his door.

The dream he'd had last night. He remembered it now. He hadn't had a nightmare like that for weeks, although there had been a time, not so long ago, when he'd had one almost every night. He'd been ill then, made himself ill because of those dreams, couldn't bear to let himself sleep. Mrs Moore from the village who came in to clean had found him asleep in the kitchen one morning, his head on the table and the dog whining, believing him dead. 'Lord,' she'd said later, 'you gave me such a turn, Sir.'

His kettle was boiling, spilling tiny beads of water, like mercury, on to the hotplate. He lifted it off and made the pot of tea. Cheap brown pot. They'd had that, hadn't they, before the Colonel died? He sat down at the table. The dog got up, shook himself and lay down again on his old mat.

'Good boy,' said Sadler.

He didn't want to think about the dream. He always

14

chose the memories of his mother with such nervous care, examining only those that gave him hardly any pain. The rest he would have kept hidden for ever, but once in a while they slipped like intruders into his sleep. Standing there, then, in the sunshine by the lych gate, waiting for the people to come, for all the people she'd ever seen, ever smiled on, ever touched, to come on that spring morning. Believing it only right, only natural that for her funeral the ugly little church would be filled, but waiting there and waiting and seeing no one come. Where were they? Charlie Ackroyd, the man she'd married, chauffeur to Milord, where was he that Saturday morning? 'Oh don't be soft, Jacky,' she herself would have said, 'of course he wouldn't come. He's been gone years now, love, and not so much as a postcard from him ever since he left.'

But Sadler had hated Charlie Ackroyd more than he'd ever hated anyone in the whole of his life. Handsome face, great mop of shiny hair, he'd met Annie Sadler when she was still just young enough to fancy. A bit thin she was and her hair never looked very nice – always untidy and wispy – but her skin was pale and clear and her grey eyes fringed with thick lashes used to look at him in quite a sexy way. But then, try as he might, he couldn't get her to bed. She kept telling him about this lover she'd had and had a child off, said she couldn't be doing with something like that all over again. And the more she pushed him away, the more Charlie Ackroyd wanted her. So he went to her room early one Sunday morning. She had the day off and was still half asleep when she opened the door, too sleepy to argue with him, forced to let him in. He sat down on a chair, didn't try to go near her in her yellow nightdress, even though he wanted to. Instead he cleared his throat like some slip of a courting lad and offered her a wedding. Annie sat down on her bed, puzzling out what was real and what just part of a dream. And Ackroyd sat there smiling, liking her confusion, noting to himself that even

15

early on a grey morning she looked rather pretty.

Milady gave the wedding her blessing, organized a little party afterwards in the servants' hall. For a month or two both of them were happy. Annie's cheeks began to bloom and she combed her untidy hair into a little bun at the nape of her neck. Ackroyd took pleasure in her so long-neglected body, preened his male feathers. Just for a few weeks he fancied he truly loved her.

Annie wrote to Jack who was working in Scarborough, asked him to spare them a little of his time. But it was two months before he could bring himself to go. He was glad – glad for her – if she was happy. But by his silence he chose to reproach her. She wrote again. So anxious now to see him, wanting his blessing on what she'd done, knowing with sadness that his love for her had never encompassed forgiveness. And was there indeed anything to forgive? Lord, Annie said to herself, why not have myself a spot of joy – after forty-three years – without the reproaches of my son?

Slowly and carefully, Sadler prepared himself for the meeting, then wrote to Annie to say he would come. But when his train came into the station Annie was standing alone on the platform. 'As fate would have it, Charlie couldn't be here, Jack. He had to take the car out, but he'll be meeting us later.'

They spent the afternoon wandering round the town. Sadler began to enjoy himself, walking round arm in arm, just the two of them. Then they went to a café where Charlie had said he'd come and Sadler ordered two teas and they waited. For more than an hour they sat drinking tea, with Annie's eyes always on the door. Then at last Sadler saw them light up and Charlie Ackroyd came in, so smart in his chauffeur's uniform, but with never so much as an apology and hardly a glance at Sadler. For Sadler was of no consequence to Charlie Ackroyd. Charlie Ackroyd didn't care twopence what Jack Sadler thought of him. Child of Annie's youth, he belonged to the past and only reluctantly did Charlie acknowledge his continuing right to exist. So Sadler went back to Scarborough and within a year Charlie Ackroyd had gone. Tired of his Annie with her thin legs and her flyaway hair. Gone because he couldn't stand the stillness in her eye. Gone to better things.

Better things! Sadler stirred his tea. He was too early for the milkman and he'd given the last drop to the dog last night. Well, he'd have to drink the tea without milk; it wouldn't be the first time. And the strong tea would make him feel better. The odd pains that crept into him in his sleep would go away once he got a warm drink inside him. And the dream? He'd forget the dream.

He rubbed his eyes. For as long as he could remember, he'd woken up early in the mornings. Habit, he supposed. A lifetime in service, up and dressed and ready with the breakfast before the master had cleaned his teeth. But now that he was old he wished he could have slept late in the mornings. So much less time to pass if you could put off waking up for an hour or two.

The Colonel, of course, with his army background, was a stickler for punctuality. 'One thing I shall make clear to you, Sadler,' he said on his second day, 'we do like things on time.'

'Naturally, Sir.'

'A house, you see, is not unlike a headquarters. Everybody does the job appointed to them at the right time and in the right place and then it all works.'

'Yes, Sir.'

'Do you understand what I mean?'

'Yes, Sir.'

'That's it then. Jolly good.'

Of course he was too old to do the job now, his hand much too unsteady. But some mornings, sitting there, just him and the dog, he longed for the great empty house to come alive again, to hear a lawn-mower out there in the sunshine, to say a word or two to the paper boy who delivered the Colonel's *Times* and Madam's *Daily Mail*, to listen to Vera, sour-faced as she made the morning coffee, complaining about something or other. It would have been nice to have had one of those conversations with Madam when he took her breakfast up. She had been so nice to him over the years, had grown, if not fond of him, at least concerned that his life wasn't too drab.

'You are happy with us, Sadler, aren't you?'

'I'm very content, Mrs Bassett.'

'You would tell me, wouldn't you, if you weren't happy with the job?'

'As I say Madam, I . . .'

'Oh I know what you *say*. It's what you feel that's important, isn't it?'

'I've never been one for staying in a position that didn't suit.'

'Well, heavens, Sadler, we didn't want you leaving! That wasn't what I meant at all. No. All I meant was if there's ever any little thing you feel isn't quite right – you know the kind of things I mean – I'd like you to think you could come and talk to me about it. You would, wouldn't you?'

'Oh I daresay I would, if it couldn't be put right without troubling you.'

'You see, we value you enormously, the Colonel and I.'

'It's nice to hear that, Madam. It's nice to know that one is giving satisfaction.'

What a pompous jackass I used to be, thought Sadler. All that dictionary language! Butlers nowadays – if there are any butlers – don't mince their words like that, surely. And yet at thirty-nine when he came to the house he'd rather enjoyed being so correct. He'd been practising for years, hadn't he? Had it dinned into him by the staff he'd worked under ever since, at Milord's house, where his mother had started as chamber-maid, he'd run errands for Mr Knightley, the butler Milord had kept at the time. But he'd lost it long ago. Don't believe I could talk like that now if I tried, he thought. Wouldn't want to. Bloody silly way to carry on – like that woman in Coronation Street who runs the pub, common as mustard, as the Colonel used to say, but so la-de-da it makes your flesh creep.

Funny though how he'd enjoyed those conversations. Used to be proud of the way he could talk so respectfully. It goes down well with the Privileged Classes, Knightley had said to his mother, and it did. The years came and went and the Colonel and his Madge got so used to the sound of that gentle, careful voice it became like a tranquillizer to them, one they couldn't do without.

'We're so lucky,' Madge said to her husband, 'to have Sadler. I'd trade all the servants I've ever employed for Sadler.'

And then as she grew older she kept saying: 'You know Geoffrey we really must leave something to Sadler in our wills.' And the Colonel thought with a kind of dread how each year he dipped further and a little further into his capital and how, when the day came, unless it came soon, there'd be nothing to leave. He always said: 'Naturally, dear, of course Sadler will be taken care of,' but somehow each time he said it he said it with less and less conviction until Madge didn't believe him any more, only wondered with some sadness where the money was slipping away. Then one morning she went to Norwich to see her solicitor who had his office in a fine old eighteenth-century house in the cathedral close, and, comfortably at ease in these surroundings, she asked him to draft her a new will. In it she stated simply that if her husband predeceased her everything she had when she died would be left to Sadler.

Madge and the Colonel had no children. Twenty-six and a virgin that day in 1900, she'd saved herself all those long years for her wedding night. They had stayed at the Savoy, such a lovely room with apricot satin bedcovers, and Madge so much in love with her lieutenant she was lying there waiting for him under the apricot before he'd taken off his trousers. He made love to her limply, thoughtlessly, the elegant room spinning round and round in his head after all that champagne at the reception. When he'd finished, as Madge lay there thinking wistfully of what her mother had told her about men being like wild beasts, he apologized.

Somehow after that, though they both tried and in spite of a real affection they found for each other, they couldn't enjoy love. For the first year they shared a bed and Madge used to ponder on how it might feel to hold a second heartbeat inside her body. But she never found out. Gratefully, thankfully, she removed herself to another room one morning and from that day decided that she wouldn't think about it again. After all, you never liked children very much, she told herself. And it was only years later when both the wars had come and gone and she began to hear the silences round her that she thought it might have been nice to talk to someone close to her, someone young enough to understand a world that now made such odd noises, someone who would explain them to her patiently without getting cross.

Anyway, there was no one. No good wishing you'd taken out a kind of insurance policy against loneliness when you hadn't. Best thing to do was give someone else the chance to be wise – for what difference could it make when the day came? And when you thought about it, there was no need to tie material possessions to love, though in her experience they always had been. Why not tie them to need? It made more sense. She wasn't so blind and old-fashioned that she couldn't see that, even if she couldn't help disagreeing with a lot of the things Mr Attlee said. But of course she knew the Colonel wouldn't understand;

it wasn't really fair to expect him to. He'd always been so keen on everything staying in the family, even when she'd reminded him that they had none. No, it would have disturbed the Colonel if she'd told him her plan. To her, it was the most rational thing she'd ever done in her life and she was rather proud of it. She thought it was sad in a way that she had to keep it to herself, but there it was.

Sadler was oddly moved by the extraordinary stroke of fortune that one June morning in 1953 made him master where for years he had been servant. Sad for her, was his first thought, that she had no one else to leave it to. He'd seen enough of Mr Knightley's Privileged Classes to know that they could be deeply hurt by the glimpse of a single possession slipping through the family net and he fancied that Madge had needed some courage to put her hand to her extraordinary testament. Had she died seven hours earlier, he would have got nothing, only the thousand pounds left to him by the Colonel. For they raced for death, the Colonel and his Madge. As vast crowds began gathering in London, sleeping out, camping on little stools near the very place where Madge had married, making flags to wave, telling their children that never, never would there be such a sight again, as they massed, expectant, long-suffering, patient, determined for that flying glimpse of the new Queen riding to her Coronation in her golden coach, Madge and the Colonel waited to die.

'Poor old things . . .' Sadler mumbled.

He didn't want to think about it, though. Not now. He often did remember it, but this morning for some reason it made him feel terribly sad. He glanced at the clock on the kitchen wall. Eight o'clock. Time moved so slowly these days. Too fast when you wanted it to stop of course, like when someone you cared to see called and then kept saying they'd have to hurry or they'd be late for something or other, but so painfully slowly when you were on your own. He sipped his tea, expecting it to be cold by now, but

21

it wasn't, it was still almost too hot to drink.

Then he remembered Mrs Moore. She'd be coming at half past eight. Only another half hour and she'd be there. Unless it was Sunday. He couldn't bear it to be Sunday and her not to come. He wasn't hungry at all, but he knew he'd ask her to make him breakfast if she came because she'd have to stay longer if she made breakfast, and there'd be time for a chat.

But Mrs Moore had said she'd have to stop coming soon. It was her legs. She couldn't get about like she used to. And the stairs – they could do dreadful things to your knees, stairs could.

'You'll have to find someone else, Mr Sadler,' she said one morning, 'it's getting too much for me.'

'Too untidy, am I? Never used to be, of course.'

'Oh no, it's not that, Mr Sadler. I just can't manage this type of work any more. I'm too old, I daresay.'

'We're all getting on. But you oughtn't to think about it. Look at the dog. You'd never say he was a hundred and five, would you! Still wags his tail.'

Sadler chuckled, but Mrs Moore only shook her head. 'Poor little old fellow.'

'Happier than I am, Mrs Moore, you mark my words. He's got me and that's all a dog needs, a good master. They don't miss the company of their own kind, do they?'

'Friends are of our making, Mr Sadler. If you . . . '

'All dead, mine.'

'Well, there's Reverend Chapman at least. He's a regular caller.'

'I never gave Jesus the time of day, Mrs Moore. Not since I was a lad and said my prayers in my mother's lap.'

'Well, I've always said, Mr Sadler, God helps those that help themselves.'

And Sadler was left on his own, pricked with the little needle of her spurious wisdom, sunk in gloom.

She won't leave, though, he told himself now. She

knows I like the companionship. Don't mind about the sweeping and polishing any more, it's the company. He thought of the house now in the same way that he thought of himself. There was so little of it left alive – most of it had been closed and shuttered long ago. What mattered was to keep going the bit of it in which he still lived – a couple of rooms, that was all. You had to keep *them* clean and aired, even if they were cold and draughty in winter. You had to let them hear the sound of voices once in a while, too. Silence accumulated otherwise, like dust.

He wondered suddenly how thick the dust was lying in his old room, the room with the child's picture. I might go and see, he thought, must've been two years since anyone went in there. And he finished his tea, glad now that he had thought of something to do. If it's not too bad, he decided, I'll sleep up there tonight. It'd make a change and it might be warmer than the Colonel's room. He got up and, trying not to wake the dog, tiptoed out into the cold passageway.

He shuffled into the hall, up the wide stairs with their loose stair-rods and their worn grey carpeting and on to the first floor landing. Then into his bedroom to find his slippers, out and up a narrower flight of stairs to where the coconut matting began. 'It's hard wearing,' Vera had said, 'but you couldn't call it smart.' Even less now. Its edges were frayed and its colours were faded and spoiled.

Sadler walked to the door of his old room, waited a moment outside it and then turned the door handle. It turned but the door didn't move. Another of those wrong decisions, Sadler thought with dismay, made a year or more ago – never thought I'd need to go in there again, no doubt, shut the door and locked it and lost the key. He cursed. Time was when all the keys of the house were kept in a tin box in the Colonel's room and carefully labelled. But that was long ago. He hadn't seen that box for years.

He turned tail and limped down the stairs. I can

remember every inch of that room, he thought, no need really to see a thing when you can remember it so well. All the same, it would have been nice to touch all the old things.

'That you, Mr Sadler?'

Oh she was there then. Couldn't be Sunday, thank Jesus.

'Mrs Moore?'

She was standing in the hall.

'I'm a bit early, Sir. Hope you don't mind.'

There was something he wanted to ask her, but he couldn't for the life of him remember what.

'I'll get on, then.'

'Yes.'

'I've not a lot of time this morning. I've got my sister staying and I promised I'd take her into town.'

'That'd be nice.'

'I like to get in before the crowds.'

'Oh yes.'

'That seems to get worse 'n worse, Saturday.'

'I suppose it would.'

And then she was gone, tying her apron round her as she bustled off, leaving Sadler standing at the bottom of the stairs.

II

Annie Sadler, sitting at her father's upright piano, liked to dream. She played with a lot of feeling, so her teacher said; a little more practice and she'd be very good. So sometimes Annie dreamed of fame and sometimes of love.

Greg Sadler, her father, was a piano tuner. He made a fair living in those distant days, when all respectable homes had a piano. December, of course, was the busiest time of year for him, when Christmas crept into sight and families began to think of the sing-song they'd have – Good King Wenceslas and God Rest Ye Merry Gentlemen and Uncle George or Aunt Beatrice playing, wrong notes and all but so good for the spirit. He'd be working twelve hours a day sometimes in the weeks before Christmas, come home sick and tired of the sound of the darned instrument, to find his daughter playing away in the front room in the dark, always Chopin and with a wrapt expression on her face. 'Lord,' he'd say crossly, 'what's wrong with supper then, Annie?'

But he spared her no love. He'd brought her up on his own and in her he had vested a formless kind of hope. She wasn't pretty of course. Never had been, even as a little girl. Her face was much too long and her hair so fine and wispy you'd fancy the wind could blow it away. But she had a stillness about her that folk found appealing. And she was all he had.

They lived in a small house in a clean little town in Suffolk that went about its business with a ponderous slowness, found a respectable response to the ringing of its

Sunday bell and prospered a little from its recently built pork pie factory. Annie liked it. By the time she was sixteen, in 1898, she recognized that to walk down its short main street was to her like being held between two familiar, comforting arms and she vowed she would never leave it. Oh she was timid all right, far too timid and shy for a girl of her age, Greg Sadler was aware of that. But to snatch her up and drop her somewhere else would have caused her such pain that he never would have suggested it, although, as her aunt declared on a visit from London, it might have done her the world of good.

She wasn't particularly clever. At school she'd done her best with the books she'd had to read, but the music lessons were all she cared about. In the summer, on hot days when all the windows were open, the whole street could hear her playing. 'I don't know,' Greg used to mutter to her as she sat there, 'what are we going to do with you, Annie girl?'

Do? In Annie's mind *doing* was never in question. She'd kept house for her father from the age of eleven when her mother had died and she could imagine no other life. One day, perhaps, the notions she had about love would crystallize and she'd choose a man to bear the burden of them. But until that day came – and somehow it seemed a long way off – she'd pray to God every Sunday to let her stay put.

Annie had loved her mother. When she died, she wanted everyone to be silent and let her just *think*, not weep or say she was sorry, but just sit quietly and think about it until she had thought it out. Silence, occasionally, was like darkness: it erased things. And once the funeral was over, the relations come and gone and the cakes eaten, Annie and Greg never spoke about it again. By doing this, they believed they would forget. The less they talked, the less they remembered; the more the silences accumulated, the more the image they wanted to rub out grew invisible.

26

When Annie was sixteen and a half, her music teacher got married. Woman of fifty, single all her life, what business had she going off and doing a thing like that? But there she was one fine morning at St Teresa's Church in her best blue silk, all the neighbours agog, hanging out of windows, and the groom, they all said, very neatly dressed and handsome for a man of his age. The town wished her well, but not without raising an eyebrow or two and everyone declared it impossible to think of a wedding gift, for what could she need at her time of life? Annie gave her a cushion cover she'd worked herself during the evenings when Greg had been too tired to let her play the piano. Then with dismay she watched her leave the town a few weeks later, bound for London.

For day after day the piano stayed closed. Greg Sadler breathed a sigh of relief, and as if to compensate for what he knew was a selfish feeling, started to tell his daughter what a sweet sight she was these days, looking so grown up now, dressing so nicely on the little money she had, and wouldn't he just know it if some young lad mightn't come along who'd take a fancy to her. But with the departure of the one person who had encouraged her, Annie's favourite dream had fled. She couldn't play any more and, though she tried, she couldn't talk to her father as they sat face to face in the evenings. She knew he was trying to cheer her up with all his compliments and she loved him for it, but it did no good. She felt her little girl's soul going brown.

Then Greg Sadler met Betsy Elkins, Annie's friend, in the main street one morning, and Betsy, all gay ribbons and pink smiles, said: 'Tell you what's happened, Mr Sadler . . .' Greg, late for a client, harassed and hot on this sunny day, stood prisoner for a full ten minutes while Betsy told him that her favourite uncle and aunt, not to mention her handsome cousin Joe, had been left a house no more than three minutes walk from her own, the little one with the yellow windows opposite the church, and wasn't it exciting they'd be moving in any day.

Escaping from her with the merest: 'That's fine, Betsy', Greg pondered this information on his hurried way to work. He would, he decided, take the opportunity of a glance at young cousin Joe, and if he liked the look of him, make sure that Annie was dressed up and looking her best the first time she met him. Not a word to Annie, of course. Let her brood over the ugly piano. For wasn't the first day of spring, arriving undreamed of in winter's cold lap, the more welcome because unannounced? Greg Sadler loved metaphors and was very proud of this one. So proud, in fact, that he wished he could have said it aloud to someone listening.

But then on the first of June, before Greg had gone to work, Betsy Elkins came tapping at the Sadlers' front door. Today was the day of the great arrival, she said, and she was so excited at the thought of their coming that she'd love her friend Annie to share it all with her, especially as couldn't she see it was a fine morning and it'd be so much fun helping them unpack their things and get everything straight and what's more she was sure they could do with another pair of hands.

When Betsy stopped for breath Annie began 'Well, Bets . . .'

'Course Annie must go.' Greg said firmly.

'Monday's usually——'

'Washing'll keep, won't it love?'

'You'll be needing a clean shirt tomorrow.'

'And a thousand pounds and a lot of other things!' Betsy laughed.

'Go *on*,' Greg said, 'go and have some fun, girlie.'

No sooner said than Betsy had caught Annie's hand and was dragging her out into the sunshine. 'We've got to go and pick some flowers,' she was saying, 'I promised my Mum that we'd be welcoming when they come . . .'

After they'd gone, Greg cursed. For what was his Annie

wearing that morning if not her old green smock she put on for housework? Why in the world hadn't he noticed and told her to go and change, to put on something that set off her nice little figure. Angry with himself, he cleared away the breakfast crocks and, unconcerned whether he'd be late for his job, set about washing them up.

Annie and Betsy filled an old basket with wild blue cornflowers and mauve scabious growing by the hedgerows where the narrow road led eastwards out of town. 'They never last,' said Annie, 'if you pick them.' But Betsy insisted, for what was more welcoming than a vase of flowers?

Then they walked back to the house with the yellow windows and Betsy, dismayed by finding the door locked, climbed in, petticoat and little brown boots in the air, through one of the windows. Then as she turned to give a hand to Annie, she remembered she'd forgotten the vase her Mum had said she could borrow. So out she climbed again, her cheeks red and shiny now because of the heat and her breath fast running out.

'You wait here,' she panted, 'in case they come. I'll go and bring the vase.'

'But Betsy . . .'

She was off down the street, flying along like a little white butterfly, almost out of sight before Annie could finish her sentence.

Annie was hot, too. She noticed that the entrance porch to the house had two little stone seats, one on either side of it, so she sat down there, grateful for the shade. What a burning summer's day it was, the kind of day you remembered when you were old. She sniffed the flowers. All their freshness would be gone in a few hours of this heat. So silly of Betsy to want to pick them. Annie put them down, to spare them the heat of her hand. Then she took off her heavy green smock, folded it up and put it under the seat. Sitting there, in her clean white blouse and her favourite

29

blue skirt, she felt quietly happy. In the shadow of the porch her wide grey eyes looked very black.

It was like this, half hidden by the brick pillars of the porch, that Joe Elkins first saw her. His head was damp with sweat from driving the horse and heavy old cart over bumpy roads and the sweat had begun to run down into his eyes, that and the strong sunlight doing their best to blind him. So, as he clambered down from the cart and caught sight of Annie sitting in the shadow, he wondered if she was really there. He rubbed his eyes and he saw her get up and come towards him, holding out some flowers.

'Good morning,' Joe said.

'I'm sorry . . .' Annie began, 'Betsy just went up to her Mum's for a vase – for these.'

'Oh?'

'She won't be more than a minute or two.'

Joe smiled. 'Left you on guard, did she?'

'In a way.' Annie felt herself blushing. 'I'm Annie Sadler.'

'Pleased to meet you, Annie Sadler. I'm Joe Elkins, cousin Betsy's cousin.'

He'd come on ahead on his own. 'Family porter, that's me,' he said nodding at the loaded cart.

'But they'll be coming on, your Mum and Dad?'

'Tomorrow afternoon. Mother can't be doing with any kind of muddle, has to have everything in its place before she'll sit down.'

He laughed. Annie looked away, knew otherwise she'd stare at him. He found the key to the front door and opened it. It led into a tiny hallway with rooms branching off and a staircase going straight up. Joe looked back at Annie who hesitated at the door.

'Come and see,' he said, amused by her shyness. 'It's quite a fine little house.'

She followed Joe from room to room. In each one he went to the window and opened it wide. 'Air and sunshine,' he said, 'that's important if a place is to be right.'

The rooms were square and small, smaller empty of furniture, and, to Annie, Joe seemed too big for the house. It wasn't that he was very tall, but he was sturdy with wide, strong shoulders and a mop of curly black hair that made his head seem large. Annie wondered how old he might be – twenty-three perhaps, even twenty-five. His arms, where his shirt was rolled to the elbow, were tanned and covered in soft brown hair. Noticing them, Annie wanted to touch them.

'What do you think, then, Annie? It's a fair little old house, isn't it?'

'Oh it's fine,' said Annie. 'My Dad and me are at the other end of town; the houses aren't as fine there.' And she smiled.

'How old are you, Annie?' Joe asked.

'Sixteen.'

'Ah.'

At that moment Betsy came back, clutching her vase, a vase much too tall and grand for the flowers they'd picked. She ran to Joe and he whirled her into the air, kissing her on both her pink cheeks.

'What a time we'll have, eh Bets!' he said.

Then they began unloading the cart, piece by bulky piece of furniture, suitcases full of linen and china and dusty odds and ends that were all brought out and laughed over. Betsy complained playfully all morning.

'Lor, Joe Elkins, anyone'd think we was dockside haulers, the way you make us fetch and carry.'

'No one else to do it, Betsy.'

'Well, what'd you have done without us?'

'Done it all on my own.'

'What conceit!'

So hot they all were by midday, and untidy and covered in dust and dirt and hungry and thirsty, that Betsy sat herself down on the bare floorboards of the front room and declared she'd lift nothing more till Joe fed and watered her. Annie flopped down beside her. 'See,' said Betsy, 'strike!'

So they sent Joe off to Mrs Bolton's General Store, sat and chatted while he was gone, even lay down flat on their backs on the dusty floor to have a rest and Betsy said she wasn't tired at all really, because if you were happy didn't Annie agree that you just didn't notice other feelings? Annie shut her eyes. She could smell the sunshine now, feel a breeze on her face, coming through the wide open window. She noticed that her mind had begun to feast on her image of Joe and that already it was constructing all the dimensions that it couldn't see, spinning a little web out from itself to him, along which she travelled like a fly.

'You are silly,' Betsy said suddenly.

Annie jumped.

'Why, Bets?'

'Well, you know what should happen? You should make Joe be in love with you.'

Annie smiled. 'He'd never be!'

'Why?'

'He just wouldn't.'

'If you married him, you'd be my cousin too, in a way.'

'So you would, Annie.'

They sat up. Joe was standing laughing in the doorway, holding a bag of groceries and a jug of cider. Annie blushed to think he'd heard their chatter, but Betsy was unconcerned.

'I was telling Annie,' she said, 'she should marry you, then my two nicest people would be in one house.'

'Know what, Bets,' said Joe, 'I do believe you always did think everyone should make their plans to suit you.'

Betsy wished she'd taken off one of her little brown boots so that she could throw it at him. 'Where's my picnic?' she whined.

'Come on,' said Joe, 'whoever heard of a picnic *inside*?'

So out they went, up into one of Farmer James's big meadows, the one where two old oak trees stood side by side in the middle, giving them welcome shade. Joe spread the food out.

'Pork pies! I might have guessed,' said Betsy.

Joe looked bewildered.

'We should have told him not to get pork pies, shouldn't we, Annie?'

Annie smiled.

'Don't you like them?' asked Joe.

'Of course we don't like them. Everyone in the whole town doesn't like them any more.'

Annie explained about the factory.

'I'd have thought you'd have heard about it,' commented Betsy. 'We're famous for that.'

Joe apologized, promised to eat the three pies himself and give them all the bread and cheese.

'That's not fair,' said Annie, 'I might try a pie, anyway, I've not had one for so long, it'd make a change, wouldn't it, Bets?'

'I'd be sick,' said Betsy, 'especially on a day like this.'

'Have a drink of cider, then,' suggested Joe, 'then you can go to sleep.'

'I don't want to go to sleep.'

'I want you to.'

'Just so you can say evil things to my friend Annie.'

'Impossible.'

'Why?'

'She's too nice.'

'How d'you know, Joe Elkins?'

'I know.'

'She's much nicer than me, everyone says so, don't they Annie?'

'Only you, Bets.'

'No. They say it inside themselves, I can hear.'

'Serve you right for eavesdropping,' said Joe, and Betsy

33

laughed. Then she cut herself a large chunk of bread and some cheese and lay down on her back while she made an elaborate sandwich of it. Annie watched her and Joe leant back against the tree, enjoying his pie and watching Annie.

He liked her shyness. There was, in his opinion, too fleeting a moment in a girl's life when she had that kind of shyness and whenever he came across it, it amused and excited him. It was, he decided, a kind of covering that could play as seductive a role as a petticoat. His man's mind judged as inconsequential the things that girls talked about, but when they didn't talk much, blushed now and then, hid the brightness of their eyes, then he found them interesting.

Annie fitted exactly the concept he had of 'girl'. Her face was long but he found it appealing, her body was enchanting – small breasts whose firmness he had already glimpsed in his mind, slim legs and neat little hips. He could imagine that Annie's tongue was rather small and pointed, that when he kissed her it would touch his nervously, reluctantly until, little by little, he'd taught it what to do.

They'd eaten most of the food. Joe had had two pies and the big loaf of bread was nearly gone. Now they drank the cider, passing the jug round from one to the other, and Annie's body was, for the first time that day, completely relaxed. She wanted to lie down, but wouldn't let herself. To lie down so near to Joe was a temptation she felt she had to fight. Like looking at him. She only allowed herself to look at him every now and then. Annie closed her eyes. The sun had moved round a bit and was now on her face. She listened to the sounds in the field, letting them fill her head like a favourite piece of music.

It was two weeks before Annie saw Joe again. So busy,

Betsy said he was, settling himself and his Mum and Dad into the house, that he'd had no time for calling, especially as he wanted to see the house straight before starting work with Mr James. Secretly, Annie was disappointed. She'd gone home very tired that Monday evening, unable to hide from her father the excitement she was feeling, confident enough that she'd be seeing Joe again very soon to tell Greg all about him. Greg beamed with pleasure as Annie recounted her day, couldn't resist saying 'Well, I'm glad something's come along to cheer you up.' And the next day, Annie put on a smarter dress than usual, just in case Joe called. But he didn't come.

The hot weather stayed. After a week of it, people in the town were beginning to grumble, just as they grumbled about the cold or the rain for most of the year. Betsy called once, to say her mother was very poorly, but not a word about Joe, except to say he was busy.

'How are they settling in?' asked Greg.

'Oh, all right, Mr Sadler. It takes a while, that do, to get things in order.'

'Well, you may tell your aunt and uncle and your cousin that if they'd like to drop by for a glass of rhubarb wine or even for one of Annie's best steak and kidneys, they'd be more than welcome.'

'I'll tell them,' said Betsy, 'but they're that busy.'

A few days later, a chilly morning surprised the town as it drew its curtains. Annie looked for her thick green smock to put on and for the first time remembered where she had left it, under the little stone seat in the Elkins's porch. She asked herself at once if she'd have the courage to walk down and collect it. She didn't know, she decided, she'd have to see.

She didn't go that day or the next, but on Sunday morning she thought, I'll go to church and make that my reason for being that end of town. It was fine again, warm but not too hot, with a sun that came and went as the clouds chose. Annie put on a brown dress, made sure her hair was as tidy as it could be and then, just as she was about to leave, heard her father say he'd fancy singing a hymn or two and that he'd come with her.

'Hurry, then, Dad, and change or you'll be late.'

'What's the time, then?'

'Twenty to.' Annie lied by ten minutes, knowing he hated hurrying.

'Oh you go then, girlie. I can't fancy rushing about on a Sunday morning. You go on.'

So she picked up her hymn-book and went out, noticing as she closed the front door that her hands were shaking.

The church was full. Years afterwards, when Annie remembered that church, she saw it always full of people who listened eagerly, sang loudly, prayed with their eyes shut. She liked to sit at the back, near the organ. 'Just so you can criticize the playing,' Greg teased. 'Oh no,' Annie said, 'I like to watch the other people.'

She sat now in a pew opposite the door, opened her hymn book and started to read through the words of the first hymn, but each time the door opened she looked up. Because, living just across the road, it had occurred to her, Joe's family might feel obliged to come, even if they weren't churchgoing people. She'd had a good look round, of course, and they weren't there yet, not that she could see. But it was only five to eleven and living so near they'd be sure to hurry in at the last minute.

But the service started and the door stayed shut. Joe hadn't come, so she'd have to make the smock her excuse for seeing him after all. Annie started to sing the hymn:

> . . . Time like an ever-rolling stream
> Bears all our sins away,
> They fly forgotten as a dream
> Dies at the opening day

Then she heard the heavy latch on the door lift again,

glanced up and saw Joe come through the door. She looked down again at her hymn-book, but the words were jumping on the page and she couldn't sing. He slipped into the pew beside her and put his broad hand over hers that held the hymn-book.

'Forgot my book,' he whispered.

Sitting at the parlour window, smoking his pipe and watching the people going into church, Joe had suddenly caught sight of Annie going down the path and he made a quick decision to put on a tie and the black jacket he kept for best and follow her in. Thinking about her as he changed, he counted almost a fortnight since the day they'd met. He'd been holding her in reserve, thinking about her now and then, letting the days pass till the right one should arrive for a second meeting. Because he was sure, was Joe Elkins, that whatever beauty he had chosen to see in Annie Sadler was being lovingly cared for and that in her mind it now existed only for him.

Feeling, smelling him standing close to her, letting her hand be held, Annie loved him. But, half afraid of where that love would take her, sensing that what she felt was unconnected with any of the notions she'd had about love as she'd sat dreaming in Greg's front room, she began to drag it on to safe soil, saw herself marrying Joe in this very church, saw her father smiling as he poured wine for them afterwards, taking Joe by the arm and telling him he was glad. She saw her dress, expensive silk from Mrs Collard's drapers shop, bought from weeks and weeks of savings, but so soft next to her skin that she hardly felt it at all . . .

The service was nearly over. The sermon had been short – as it always was because the rector had varicose veins and didn't like to stand for long, especially in summer. Annie hadn't heard a word of it. And Joe, too, had been absorbed by Annie, watching her head as she knelt down to say prayers, noticing how very silently her body moved. Once, during the sermon, he'd turned to her and

37

seeing her eyes all ashine had felt a sudden dread and turned away.

But he wanted her. Not for a year or more had he felt as urgent a desire for a girl as he felt for Annie Sadler. He believed she was his discovery and that this gave him an absolute right to her. For hadn't he, in seeing her beauty, made it flower? No other man had ever seen in her what he saw, he was sure. They had passed her in the street, at the market, in church, but not looked, not *seen*. He'd have to be careful, of course, not to fill her head with romantic dreams, but he'd have her all right, if he jostled time a little. Her eyes told him she fancied herself in love. All that had to be done now was to weave a labyrinth where, believing herself lost, she'd run to him.

Outside the church, he put his hand under her elbow and they made silent progress up the street, not touching after they left the churchyard, nor looking at one another.

'I'll be seeing you, Annie,' said Joe when they reached Annie's door, and he walked off quickly before she could ask him when.

For Annie the summer now lay in abeyance. July came, with another spell of hot weather, but Annie stayed indoors mostly in the dark parlour. She believed now that she had been wrong: Joe had felt nothing for her. So silly of her, so like the plain virgin she was to have interpreted his friendliness as love. Each morning when she got up, early these days, woken by the sun, she took off her nightdress and looked critically at her body in the mirror, wondered how it could be changed to fulfil the role God in His unwisdom had fashioned it for. Only a week or two ago, on the day of the picnic, she had been quite pleased with it, felt it move with joy. Now it angered her, thin straight thing that it was, feeling passion and yet exciting none, and the future made her feel afraid. She had been cheated; she would grow old untouched.

Her head began to fill with plans. She would try once

more. She would go down to fetch the smock one evening when Joe was home. She would buy a new dress, she'd ask her father for the money. Then she put the plan aside. Joe would know she had only come to see him. He would despise her. And what if, after all, Joe had a girlfriend? She might be there when Annie called, sitting at the family table, accepted, loved. She might be beautiful. No, Annie wouldn't call in. She'd tell Betsy about the smock and Betsy would tell Joe and he would bring it up one evening, while there was still daylight enough to go for a walk round the town. But then why indeed should Joe choose to take her for a walk, and even if he did, what could she say to him?

Greg Sadler noticed a sullenness in his daughter and he understood the reason for it. He was too wise to think of meddling, too loving not to feel sad. If things continued as they were, it might be better after all to send Annie to London. She could be found domestic work there and her aunt would take care of her and help her to settle down. But Greg hated to think of sending her away. For the first time for some weeks he began thinking about his wife, wishing she were there so that Annie, who kept some things secret from him, might talk to her.

Across the road, Betsy's mother still lay in her sick-room. The doctor was very worried, so Greg had heard, and, looking up at her window with its drawn curtains day after day Greg believed she was dying. He went to see her. He took her some of his wallflowers.

'They're lovely, dear,' she said. 'That's always been one of my favourites.'

'How are you feeling, Mrs Elkins?'

'Oh not so bad, dear, thank you. A little better today. It's my chest, you see.'

She was very white – yellow white – and her eyes were tired. 'I have a bother sleeping,' she said.

Betsy was sitting by the window. No ribbons or smiles

39

today, only a wan little face and nervous hands twisting a pocket handkerchief in her lap.

'How's your cousin, Betsy?' Greg asked her. 'Settled in yet?'

'Oh yes,' Betsy said, 'he's working for Farmer James.'

'He's been to see you, has he?' Greg asked Mrs Elkins.

'What, love?'

'Joe. Cousin Joe. He been up to see you?'

'Oh yes.'

'He comes every evening,' said Betsy.

Greg sat down next to Betsy. He was tempted, in that quiet room, to tell her about Annie. But he stopped himself. Don't you meddle, Greg Sadler, he told himself. He stayed till he fancied Mrs Elkins was getting tired, stayed and chatted about the things in his garden. Then he got up and left. On the way downstairs he shuddered.

Then when he got home, Annie greeted him with a smile – the first smile for days, it seemed to Greg.

'Joe Elkins called while you were out, Dad. He brought my smock.'

The smock had been quite useful to Joe. He had let a good fortnight pass after he'd seen Annie in church and then judged the time right for a visit. He knew it was no good letting girls like Annie Sadler come home to meet his parents. Hardly into the front room and they began to get notions about becoming part of the family. That had happened once before, with a publican's daughter in Colchester called Faith. And you couldn't take them presents or be really nice to them or you'd find you'd get no more than a kiss without a great promising of eternal love and fidelity. And just to say those things made you feel old. But he wanted to see Annie. He thought he'd ask her would she fancy dropping by for a glass of wine after supper one evening. His parents spent most evenings with Betsy's mother nowadays, taking it in turns to sit with her. Joe would tell Annie that he was lonely.

40

And once the idea of asking her to come and see him had entered his mind, he found he didn't want to wait any longer. Annie had been there in his mind ever since the day of the picnic. He prided himself that he had handled the situation with care, nice to her one day, gone the next. By now, he told himself, she wouldn't know where she was with him. So the time had come to call.

When she answered the door to him, she had her apron on and her hair was wet, tied up in a towel. She blushed when she saw him, started to take her apron off.

'May I come in, Annie?'

'Of course. My Dad's over at Betsy's, though.'

'I came to see you. I found this.' He held out the smock. 'Isn't Betsy's, so I reckoned it should be yours.'

'Yes. I left it in your porch, didn't I? Won't you come in? My Dad's made me a fire in the front room, to dry my hair.'

Joe sat down in one of the comfortable armchairs. Annie knelt on the hearthrug and began to unwind the towel from round her head.

'You've been working hard, then?'

'Oh, fairish.'

'He's quite a bit of land, hasn't he, Mr James?'

'Two hundred acres. I'll be busier come harvest time.'

'I love the harvest.'

'You could come up and give me a hand then.'

She looked up at Joe. Her wet hair was a dark, tangled mass. Joe likened her to a solemn little doll with twine for hair. He leant forward and twisted a strand of it round his finger, then he put his face very close to hers and began in a whisper: 'Tell you what, Annie, I've been wanting to come and see you for a long, long time. And I was thinking, if you wouldn't mind a bit of a walk one evening, it'd be nice to drink a glass of wine with you at home. Would you like that? You see, you know Betsy's Mum's very poorly and needs someone with her all the time, so my

41

mother and father are up with her most evenings and I'm on my own . . .'

Annie was very hot. She wanted to move away from the fire.

'Yes, I'll come,' she said.

She went to Mrs Collard's the next day and bought herself a new dress. Blue, with a tight bodice. She couldn't pay for it and, knowing she'd soon have to lie to her father, couldn't ask him for the money. She paid ten shillings down and promised Mrs Collard the rest within two months.

Then one evening she cleared away the supper things and went and put her dress on. She had bought some matching ribbon and she made a little knot of her hair at the nape of her neck and tied the ribbon round it. She came downstairs and tiptoed to the front door, then called out to her father that she was going over to Betsy's and went out before he could answer her.

It had rained that afternoon and it was quite chilly outside, but the clouds had moved on, uncovering stars in their wake. There was scarcely anyone about as she hurried down the main street, only old Harry Brown, Mr James's bailiff, sitting on the stone cattle trough, sucking his pipe.

'Evenin', Annie,' he mumbled.

'Evening, Mr Brown.'

But on past him, not stopping for a chat, knowing old Harry Brown would have liked a chat, living alone as he did. But walking faster, almost running with her heart racing under the tight bodice of her dress. Down to the Post Office, past the line of cottages at the end of the street, past the rectory with its lovely iron gates, skirting the churchyard railings and then crossing the road, noticing a light in Joe's parlour window behind the red curtains and feeling suddenly very cold, starting to wish she hadn't come.

'You've come, then?'

Annie was motionless outside the door, standing face to face with Joe and neither of them moving. Then Joe smiled.

'Come in. It's cold out, isn't it?'

He put a hand on her arm, bringing her inside.

'You're shivering.'

'Oh it was quite chilly walking down. I didn't expect it or I'd have put a coat on.'

'Well, I've got a fire going.'

He took her hand and led her into the lighted parlour. The apple logs he was burning made such a strong smell that Annie's girl's mind likened it to incense, suddenly saw herself as the novice, head bowed, her mind a whirl-wind of prayer, being led step by step to God. But what a fanciful notion, that! And how silly Joe would think her if he knew.

He handed her a glass of sweet wine. Tiny little glass. Then he poured one for himself and gave her a smile as he took the first sip. Annie's hand was shaking as it held her glass. She spilt a drop of wine on to the velvet covered couch as she tried to drink.

'Look what I've done.'

'Won't show, will it? Same colour as the chair.'

Joe sat down on the couch and rubbed the drop of wine with his finger.

'See.'

Annie smiled. Joe held out his hand to her.

'Come and sit down by me, Annie.'

She sat down and Joe looked at her. He had been right. There was a kind of beauty in her. With the firelight – or perhaps it was the walk she'd just had – giving her cheeks a fine colour, her face looked rounder, softer. Joe closed his eyes. He couldn't talk to her, didn't even want to try. And yet he was conscious of the silence, of the clock ticking and knew that unless he talked to her she might be afraid, she might be so afraid that she would leave, just drink her wine and go home.

She was staring at the fire. Joe put his glass down and turned to her, taking her two hands, lifting her glass from the tight grip she had on it. Then he put his arms round her and kissed her forehead. Tiny beads of sweat glinted there and in the parting of her hair. He held her against him for a moment, then he kissed her mouth, tasting wine on her tongue. She clung to him, not moving, just clinging with her arms round his neck and her eyes wide open, staring into the firelight, full of wonder. Joe carried her gently off the couch and laid her down on the rug in front of the fire. Looking at her eyes, he felt afraid, dreaded to think what thoughts spun behind them, what fancies she lay conjuring. But he couldn't stop now. He had to have her now.

He undid her bodice, quickly, deftly, not looking at her face, then brought his head down between her breasts. So terribly still she lay, seeming to move when he looked again at her with the firelight dancing over her but not moving. Only her little hands clutching at the shirt on his back.

'I won't hurt you, Annie,' Joe whispered. 'I promise I won't hurt you.' Promise her anything, he thought, promise her his soul, all for this moment.

'Joe!' Annie cried, 'say you love me.'

So he did.

On the last day of July, Betsy's mother died. Annie was there, sitting with Betsy, arm-in-arm by the window. They were talking in low voices, Betsy telling Annie about the job she was taking, working for Mrs Collard at ten shillings a week.

'It's quite good money, you know,' she was saying, 'and it'll be quite fun, won't it, doing a proper job?'

Mrs Elkins was lying on her back, sleeping. Her breathing was very loud. Then Betsy came to the end of her sentence and the two girls turned to look out of the window. It was the middle of the morning and very quiet in the street. But almost at the same moment they became aware of a sudden total silence. Betsy turned and looked at the bed, then buried her face in Annie's shoulder.

'Annie, she's dead! I can't look, Annie, help me!'

'It's all right, Bets.'

Annie cradled her friend's head, looked over it to the sleeping woman. She seemed exactly the same. Her eyes were shut and her mouth was open. Her breath was gone, that was all.

Annie led Betsy from the room. 'Mr Elkins, please come!' she called.

They buried her a few days later, all the men in their Sunday black, and Joe, his hair cut for the occasion for some reason, looking much as he had looked that day in church. But not a word to Annie. Just a nod when he saw her standing there with her Dad. The merest nod, not even a smile. Annie's heart was cold. For just a few days Joe had been her lover, and now he had found another girl.

Greg knew. He had never asked any questions, never once inquired, when he found Annie didn't go to Betsy's house, where she went in the evenings looking neat and pretty. She'll tell me in her own time, he thought. But he'd met Joe a couple of times and had been struck suddenly by the size of him, much too big and broad he seemed for Annie. Joe was very friendly, very polite to him and told him on the second meeting: 'Annie and me's best of friends, daresay you heard, Mr Sadler.' Greg said he had.

And when it was over, Greg attached no blame anywhere. If that was the way things had happened, then that was what they'd have to settle for. There was no changing those kind of things, no going back.

45

The death of Mrs Elkins seemed to cast a shadow on the street. By the time August was half through, autumn winds shuffled the plane trees. A summer that had visited them early, early left. And Annie, because of the cold she said, took one of her mother's old shawls out of mothballs and began wrapping herself in it.

Then one morning in September Greg came down to the kitchen to find Annie sitting there, her face white and sweating, her body shaking with sobs. She had been sick on the floor.

'Lord, Annie love, why didn't you call, girlie?'

Greg took out his clean handkerchief, ran it under the cold tap and, putting his arm round Annie, very gently wiped her face.

'I'm sorry,' Annie sobbed, 'I'll clean it up.'

'You'll do nothing of the kind, darling. You'll come straight upstairs and into bed.'

Greg helped her up, almost lifting her. She leant heavily against him as they went upstairs and she couldn't stop crying. Somehow, the comfort she drew from her father's safe arm weakened her and she wept uncontrollably.

Tucked up in her narrow bed, she closed her eyes and her crying gradually ceased. Greg stroked her forehead.

'You just lie there quiet a minute while I clear up downstairs, then I'll bring up a pot of tea and we can have it together.'

'You'll be late for work, Dad.'

'No work to do today,' Greg lied, 'one job late this afternoon.'

'You're dressed for work.'

'Just so as I won't have to change later on.'

Annie smiled. Then she summoned breath.

'Dad . . .' she began.

'What is it, love?'

'I'm having Joe's baby.'

Greg looked at her, wondering what courage she'd

needed to tell him. 'So that's what it is,' he said, 'wrapping yourself up in your Ma's shawl.'

He made tea and brought it up to her. They talked and made plans, grateful for the tea that steadied them both and Annie knew that whatever might happen to her, she was fortunate in being Greg's child.

Greg's kindness, his cheerfulness, even the little jokes he occasionally made about Annie looking much prettier now that she was fat, sustained her through the tedious winter. He was very busy round Christmas time of course, as he was each year, but the extra money he earned went to buy things for the baby – a wooden cot and a little blanket, a couple of shawls and some flannel nightgowns. By the time the New Year came Annie looked forward to the April that would give her her child. Joe was remote now, gone long ago, left the house with the yellow windows as soon as Betsy told him about Annie's child.

'What else can I do, Bets?' he asked.

'You could marry Annie.'

'Oh Betsy.'

'Why not? Why couldn't you?'

'I've someone else now.'

'To marry?'

'Maybe.'

'Yes or no?'

'She'll come with me and we'll see.'

She was called Arabella. She followed Joe to a job on a farm in Essex and in February her grandfather died and left her some money. So Joe deliberated a week or two and then decided to marry her. All the Elkins made the long trip down for the wedding, but it was worth it, they said, because the bride and groom looked a picture.

As March began, the first snow of the winter fell.

'You'd call that spring, March, wouldn't you?' Betsy remarked one morning when she called to see Annie on her way to work. 'And just look at it.'

47

But Annie liked the snow. Not to walk about in any more, just to watch, to sit at the parlour window in the warm house and watch it falling and drifting. She'd open the window from time to time and throw out crumbs for the birds.

Then, doing her shopping one morning, Annie slipped on the icy pavement and fell down, the potatoes in her basket rolling away into the gutter. She scrambled to her feet, helped by passers by and a little boy who appeared from nowhere who went round and round picking up all the potatoes. Annie was all right, only a bit white from the shock. But by the time she got home, the pains had begun, so she wrapped herself up again and trod a careful path to the doctor's house. She was shaking, with fear mostly, she decided, or from shock, she didn't know which. And the doctor was enigmatic; his face told her nothing.

'How many weeks is it?'

He found his own answer by consulting a green card in one of his files. 'More than probable it'll be all right,' he said.

When Greg came in from work, the house had an unfamiliar smell about it, like disinfectant. And it was deathly quiet.

'Annie!' he called. But there was no answer. Then someone came tiptoeing down the stairs, a smiling fat woman in a blue overall.

'Ssh,' she said. 'She's sleeping now.'

Greg sat down on the uncomfortable chair in the hall. 'You mean . . .?'

'Yes. The baby's fine. Six and a half pounds. A boy.'

'Oh,' said Greg, 'oh.'

Not such a god-forsaken world, then, for little Jack Sadler's beginnings. A young mother who kissed him often and looked after him with infinite care, and a kindly man, aging a bit now, but still earning enough to keep the family going, who sat him on his knee and laughed to

48

make him laugh. He was warmed and fed, he was given a plaything or two, he had a little patch of grass to crawl on. If he could have remembered his first months, he would have counted them happy. Annie was the centre of his universe, but Greg's was the gentle hand that kept the universe spinning. Greg knew that without him, mother and child would have been cast helplessly adrift.

This thought began to nag and worry him. They had no savings. Only eighty pounds in the bank, that was all. And they didn't own the house they lived in, had paid rent for it all those years. No amount of thinking of it as theirs could make it so. Greg began to lie awake at nights, blaming his lack of foresight. I never thought, he accused himself, not far enough ahead. We could have saved years ago when things weren't so dear and bought a place, but I'd never manage it now.

He began to travel greater distances each week, to find more work. He told Annie they should cut down on things for themselves, think of the future. But Annie's world had stabilized once more. Joe was gone, but she was watching her baby grow and she was perfectly happy. She refused to think of what the future might hold.

'What's the sense in it, Dad? We're well now and living, aren't we? And whatever happened, I'd manage.'

Greg had nightmares about her. He saw her carrying her baby in the old grey shawl and begging in the street. And one by one his real worries seemed to accumulate. Supposing I go deaf, he thought, I couldn't carry on if I was deaf. And he took himself to the doctor's to have his hearing tested.

'You must expect a certain loss,' the doctor told him. 'You're sixty, aren't you? Bound to be a certain loss at your age.'

And that was all he could say, nothing to reassure him, nothing to take away this particular fear. And so it grew.

The same year, 1901, Queen Victoria died. People

wept. And one morning in a big house where Greg arrived to tune the grand piano, he noticed that the whole household were wearing little black armbands.

'A death in the family?' Greg asked the butler.

'Oh no,' the man explained, 'it's for Her Majesty.'

Greg nodded, felt ashamed just for an instant that he hadn't got one on, and yet thought to himself how remote they all must have been from the tiny, plump Queen in her widow's mantillas. Never even seen her, probably, unless they'd gone with the crowds to the Jubilee or to a state opening of Parliament. And yet they mourned, kitchen maids and all. He supposed that the death of Victoria made them feel insecure, they wore their armbands like a uniform, proud to be soldiers of her army and crossing the line of the twentieth century in uncertainty. Greg felt sad for them. What wouldn't he have given to cross over into a new age with years of vigour and work inside him. But he was old. His era was over.

And he couldn't work well any more, with all this worry. He stood at the piano with his ear pressed down, tapping and listening, tapping and listening, listening but not hearing, not like he used to, hearing with a certain loss, normal at his age, quite normal . . . But it wasn't just sound that was slipping away, it was his life.

As he sat there looking at the ivory keys, he tried to direct the rage he felt towards himself. For where else could he spend it? Not with God. God was a doctor he had never been able to afford. The door had stayed shut. Other patients came and went and sometimes they came out smiling. But not him. He cursed himself over and over for what he had failed to do. Music might have saved Annie, he thought now. Why hadn't he helped her and encouraged her, found her a new teacher? Where might she be now, had he done that?

So Greg shouldered a burden of guilt, a burden he'd never thought would be his to carry. He had always been

50

so certain, so wise, he believed, so sure he was doing and saying, undoing or not saying, all for the best. Just shows, he thought.

For what could his Annie do? She was skilled at nothing but her music and it was a long time now since she had practised. She wasn't even a very passable cook. Couldn't lay a fancy table. And her sewing, they'd taught her sewing at the school, but it had never been a thing she was competent at. She might find work in a shop, like Betsy, but whatever would she do with little Jack? I'm sorry, dear, Mrs Collard would say, I'd like to take you on, but a little one of that age, grubby fingers into all my braids and elastics . . . No, I'm sorry, Annie, but I couldn't have the liability . . .

Greg played. One of the gentle, familiar Chopin waltzes Annie had dreamed over. Not much more than two years ago, was it, that he'd listened to her playing it? Or was it three? That day when her music teacher had got married – how long ago was that? He didn't know. It seemed to Greg that a whole lifetime had passed since then.

III

'I don't remember my grandad, you know,' said Sadler. 'Funny.'

He was back at the kitchen table, on his second cup of tea – a cup of tea that tasted so much nicer because Mrs Moore had made a pot with proper tea leaves and sat there with him drinking it.

'Why's that, Mr Sadler?'

'Don't know. Remember other things from that time. The bit of garden. Absolutely square. I'm sure it was absolutely square.'

'Well, I expect it would be, wouldn't it, in a terrace. They make them like that, don't they?'

'But not my old Gran'pa, though I often think it might come to me one day, what he looked like.'

'You were telling me, Sir, when he died . . .'

'I was three, I think. Or four. Perhaps I was three-and-a-half. Halves are important to kids, aren't they? They – she – told me afterwards. It was summertime.'

'More tea, Mr Sadler?'

'Oh yes. Yes. "Thank God for Tea." That's what Vera used to say. She didn't have much to thank God for.'

Mrs Moore didn't like it when Sadler mentioned God. She rebuked him often, with her top lip drawn in. And Sadler often gave way to the temptation to tease her about 'your friend Jesus', thinking to himself: don't know why I do it really, when it hurts her. But it amused him.

'Oh I tell you what, Mrs Moore . . .' Sadler remembered the lost key.

'What, Sir?'

'The rooms on the top landing. I was going to have a look up there this morning, but the room was locked.'

'Which room, Mr Sadler?'

'It was the room I had, you see. In the Colonel's day, it was my room.'

'Which one was it, Sir?'

'The second to the left of the back stairs, looks out over the orchard.'

'Well, I go in all the rooms quite regularly to dust cobwebs. I don't remember any being locked.'

'I locked it, I think. A long time ago. Probably about two years ago.'

'You couldn't have done, Sir. I must have cleaned in there a fair few times since then. That's what you said, wasn't it? You told me when I came you wanted all the rooms dusted from time to time.'

'Yes. It's just . . .'

He could summon no recollection, none whatsoever, of putting the key away. But perhaps he *had* decided one day not to go in there any more. Because in that room, it seemed to him, all the past was held.

'It's just that lately, I find I . . . being on my own . . . have to think about something, you know. There's the dog, you'll say, won't you? All his little needs to be attended to. I'm not very good with the dog any more. I forget things. I forget what time he's supposed to eat. Just old age, isn't it? But I tell you what you've got a storeful of when you're old – the past. The longer you hang on, the bigger the store gets.'

'Well, I always say some things are best forgotten.'

'I daresay that's true. Bet you enjoy thinking about when you were a girl.'

'I'm too busy, Mr Sadler, for that kind of thing.'

'Are you? Too busy, are you? Well, that's good. There are plenty of days when I'd like to be busy.'

Mrs Moore had finished her tea. She was looking at the kitchen clock.

'I must get on. I'll be late for my sister.'

'Oh have some more tea, Mrs Moore.'

'Never more than two, dear. It's bad for the veins to drink too much tea.'

'I'd like another cup.'

'Help yourself, Sir. Just leave the pot and I'll wash it up before I go.'

Sadler finished the pot. Thank God for Tea. Hardly a week in her scurrying life when Vera hadn't blessed her Maker for giving her that. Nowadays, Sadler thought, it was the kind of saying they printed on the front of T-shirts. But Vera wouldn't have understood that.

Vera had always reminded Sadler of a chicken, from that first evening when he talked to her – scrawny neck, bony, yellowish arms and long fingers that pecked at things when she was nervous, hairpins that fell out round the house like moulting feathers. With her German name and her Cockney accent, nobody ever knew where she came from, only that she'd been head kitchen maid at a Mrs Burgess's before coming to Madge.

Betty asked her one evening: 'Tell us about your old man, Vera.'

She hadn't looked up from her knitting.

'I don't talk about 'im, Betty.'

And she never did. In all those years Sadler had never learned his Christian name.

Sadler watched Mrs Moore begin to bustle about. He remembered now, with dismay, that he'd meant to ask her to cook him some breakfast. He'd forgotten and now it was too late. Of course he wasn't really hungry. There was no worm eating for him in his belly. He believed he could have nothing all day and not notice.

'It's a lovely day,' Mrs Moore said.

'Cold, wasn't it, coming up?'

54

'Yes, a bit nippy. Frost all right last night.'

'Snaps the heads off the crocuses.'

'Oh no. They're a picture down the drive. If I were you, I'd get out on a day like this. You could go and have a look at the crocuses.'

'Are the daffs out?'

'Won't be long.'

Sadler nudged the sleeping dog with his foot. The dog didn't stir.

'Do him good, a walk.'

'Do *you* good, I wouldn't wonder.'

He hadn't been out for days. Too cold. He had felt like he felt when he was ill, glad to sit still near a fire, sit still and let his body rest. The thought of bundling it up in an old coat, boots and a scarf and sending it out to totter on the frozen ground was unbearable. He'd begun to wonder if he'd ever go out again. But it was nice to see a sun for once, and it was a long time since he'd been down the drive, he might enjoy it.

'I think I will go out.'

'I would, Sir.'

'I'll take the dog.'

'That's it.'

'Better get dressed up, hadn't I? Catch my death like this.'

'Finished with the tea, then?'

'Yes.'

He got up. He made his way back up the stairs to the Colonel's room. There was quite a feeling of warmth in it now because he'd left the electric fire on. It was a well insulated room, with all those cupboards, and the sun was now shining on the carpet and over the bed in great yellow squares.

There had been a time, when he was very small, he supposed, when he had expected the sun to be more or less everywhere inside a room, like it was outside, and it puzzled him that it only seemed to come in in squares. And why, more distressing still, was there always dust in a sunbeam? He'd been afraid of dust. He didn't know where it came from but whenever he saw any he'd imagined it growing like a fungus, piling up higher and higher until it smothered things. It might have been because his mother had stolen *Great Expectations* from the library at Milord's house and read it to him, a little bit every night when they were in bed. And he had been terribly, mortally afraid of Miss Havisham and the ghastly room where her wedding breakfast lay mouldering. Usually when Annie read him books – and she did this quite often, taking one carefully from the library shelves, hiding it under her mattress and then slipping it back when they'd finished it – he wanted to *be* the boy or the man in the story, but after seeing Miss Havisham's dusty room he never wanted to be Pip.

Sadler dressed carelessly, noting but untroubled that from day to day he put off having a bath. Old men look dirty, even when they're scrubbed and powdered, that was his view, and he and the dog could live quite happily with the smells his body harboured. Anyway, it certainly didn't matter what he put on: old viyella shirt – the Colonel's or his? Baggy trousers, brown corduroy with whole furrows worn away on the bottom; his thickest socks, and the one nice thing he owned in the way of clothing – his fawn lambswool cardigan, knitted for him by Mrs Moore and her sister, one side each. He looked at himself in the mirror, felt uneasily that he ought to shave if he was going out. He might meet the postman or the milk delivery van or even Lady Grainger from Dale Farm bringing his eggs in her Range Rover. But he couldn't stand the thought of shaving. It hurt him more than it tidied him up. It was as if the skin on his face was getting softer and softer.

He shuffled downstairs once again. He could hear Mrs Moore hoovering in the drawing room and, as always, he found the noise pleasing. He often wished someone would start hoovering at night, when he couldn't sleep in the deathly quiet that held him. He believed it would have comforted him.

He picked up the dog's lead which he kept on a table in the hall and as he saw it remembered that he hadn't given the dog the food he'd promised him. Not even a biscuit or a worm pill. But the dog still dozed, warm by the Aga, uncaring.

'Come on,' said Sadler.

The little clump began to wag.

'I'll get you a drink and then we'll go out.'

He picked up the chipped yellow bowl inscribed DICK in black letters. Dick wasn't the dog's name; the dog had never had a name. Dick had been the name of Tom's dog.

Tom. Sadler filled the bowl with cold water and set it down. The dog trotted up and began lapping. Tom was back in Sadler's thoughts. He watched the dog drink. No wonder the little chap peed a lot.

'Hurry up,' said Sadler. And the clump twitched at the sound of his voice.

Leading off the kitchen was what had been a pantry. Now Sadler kept his boots and the Colonel's old shooting mac in there, ready to hand when he felt like going out. Like all the Colonel's clothes, the mac fitted him well; it was six inches too long, that was all. But he enjoyed wearing it. Dressing in all the Colonel's old things had become part of his life. Boots on and the mac and a navy blue scarf round his throat, an old walking stick to lean on and he was ready to go.

He opened the door and the dog followed him out into the cold. More cold, even with the mac on, than he'd bargained for and the grass still crunchy with frost. But the garden looking wonderfully neat under its white coating, a bit like it used to be when the lawns were flat as billiard tables with all their edges straight as a knife and not a molehill to be seen.

The sky was a blinding blue, too bright to look up at. The laurels that hedged the back garden displayed a garish green plumage among the old dark leaves and there were tight, coffee coloured buds on the chestnut trees. The dog went ahead, sniffing. You wouldn't have called it a scamper: the animal's short legs were too rheumaticky for that, it was more of an amble, a little stiff trot. Sadler followed, leaning a bit on the stick, but now he was used to the cold, glad to be out, glad that the green his feet trod was his.

He'd always wondered how it would feel to own things that grew. Used to watch old Madge going round with her pruning scissors, snip, snip, snip, hers to cut and shape as she pleased. And the Colonel poisoning daisies with an orange plastic tool like a syringe.

Madge, delighted one morning by the sight of her garden under her window, felt a little ashamed, wanted to share it. There was so much of it, after all.

'So feel free, Sadler, to walk in the garden whenever you like.'

'That's very kind of you, Madam.'

'You could even have a little plot of your own if you'd like, to grow things. You could grow some strawberries, couldn't you? I know Wren would help you. He made things grow in the Middle East, you know, in *that* soil! We used to marvel. Green fingers the Colonel always said.'

Sadler didn't know about green, but gnarled they certainly were, Wren's old hands. He and Wren selected a little plot, about the size of an allotment, on rough ground next to the orchard, ground that had been left to sprout its tangle of nettles and weeds because nobody had been able to decide whether to plant apple trees on it or level it off and grow flowers.

'This'll do grand,' Wren said, 'there's good soil under there. Needs clearing, that's all.'

They didn't want to bother the gardeners. So busy they

always were with their lawn mowers and their edgers and their little boxes of seedlings, and they never came into the house. It was as if, like certain species of birds, they were afraid to leave their camouflage.

But in one season, it became Wren's garden, not Sadler's. The old man spent the whole of the war digging and planting there, kept repeating for some reason that, with times as they were, it was important to use soil wisely. Once or twice he whispered that 'the day', when it came, wouldn't find him unprepared, referring obliquely to his neat rows of radishes and feathery parsley. But no one ever really knew what he meant, nor did 'the day' ever come, as far as anyone could tell. And then as Hiroshima burned, Wren died. It was as if the bomb had hit him.

Sadler had always liked Wren. The old man had found Christian names very difficult, even his own. He preferred to call other people 'Sir' – an army legacy, of course – and he told Sadler one day that he thought of himself not as Harold, which was his name, but as 1797074, his army number. Sadler would have liked Wren to call him Jack. Their servant status was just about equal and they were friends, weren't they? And no one called him Jack any more. But somehow Wren never managed it and so they always spoke to each other in this odd, formal way.

Wren was born in Lancashire. Joined the army to escape his parents' drab home. Always an unkempt little boy, once in the army he affected a smartness of appearance, a neatness immaculate enough to gladden the heart of the most meticulous drill sergeant. It was as if he spent the rest of his life making amends for his grubby beginnings. The role of batman to the Colonel was one Wren had loved and the Colonel grew attached to him. It seemed only right that Wren should be given a part in the Colonel's retirement, and what could be a more fitting reward for all those years of buffing and polishing than a car, with its flashes of chromium to shine? The fact that

59

Wren wasn't a good driver (he'd learnt much too late) never bothered the Colonel or Madge either. They were getting on and they liked going slowly.

Thinking about Wren, Sadler turned right at the east side of the house instead of coming round in front of it to go down the drive. The lawn (you couldn't call it a lawn any more, though, it was just 'the grass' now) sloped upwards away from the house to a tattered beech hedge dividing it from the orchard and the piece of waste ground that had been Wren's allotment. Sadler reached the hedge, puffing.

'I wouldn't give you nowt for beech stuck in like that,' Wren had criticized. 'Too damned untidy, the way them leaves hang on.' But the yews, the great dark shoulders, they gave him pleasure.

There was a wooden gate set in the hedge. Sadler undid the latch and went through.

'Come on then!' he called to the dog.

Weeds and brambles had long since reclaimed the patch that Wren had tended. In the summer the nettles sprang up shoulder high. But whenever he stared at that bit of ground, Sadler always saw Wren with one muddy wellington pressing on his spade or squatting, hunched over, his careful fingers making little beds for his seedlings. Sadler had never done much in the way of work there, only one summer – at Tom's request.

'Couldn't you sow some flowers?'

'Well, it's more of a vegetable garden, Tom.'

'They'd grow, wouldn't they?'

'Yes.'

'You can buy these packets of flowers in Woolworths.'

'Seeds.'

'I dunno. They got pictures of flowers on.'

So they went with Wren in the car to Norwich and in Woolworths Tom chose a packet of shirley poppies and a packet of larkspur and Wren grudgingly granted Tom and Sadler a few feet of earth to sow them in. They came up – to Tom's delight – but he complained that the colours weren't the same as on the packet. And he never wanted to pick them.

'Bet they'd die, wouldn't they?'

Sadler went into the orchard. He remembered that when he went for walks with Tom, the boy nearly always ran on ahead, shouting.

The billeting officer, Miss Mary Reader, always thought of herself as a Socialist. She volunteered for the job of billeting officer late in 1939, after she discovered what was happening in her own village to the first trainloads of evacuee children from London.

Mrs Dart, who lived next door to her (a smaller, more rickety door, but nonetheless side by side with Miss Reader's in The Street) had taken in two – a brother and sister from Hackney. With these additions, she now had to find food and clothing for a family of seven, all on Jim Dart's nurseryman's wage of £6. 14s. 6d a week. Miss Reader watched the Darts. She watched how proper walking shoes and woollen socks and macs were found for the Hackney children. She saw Jim Dart bring home comics for them. She noticed that most evenings when he came back from work, he'd take them off with him for a walk with Ross, the collie. She watched how their two pale faces acquired little dabs of colour.

Then she began to inquire which other families in the neighbourhood had taken on London children. Mrs Doughty at the shop didn't know, although she said she'd seen 'some unfamiliar faces', but the rector's wife, herself a billeting officer, said: 'Oh, response has been wonderful, we've placed several children in Hentswell village alone. And of course, it's working so well: just the right kind of people have come forward.'

But Miss Reader wanted to see for herself. It seemed to

her that even if it was fortunate that the poor of the countryside opened the doors to the poor of London, it was unfair. The guilt she had felt about not being poor herself bobbed to the surface once more and she spent an anxious night thinking up ways to expiate it. The following morning, she enrolled as a billeting officer.

Miss Reader's father was a publisher and her mother, ten years older than her husband, had been a friend and colleague of Mrs Pankhurst. She was now an authoress of minor importance. The Readers lived in Russell Square, in a fine old house where they would die they swore, when the bombs fell, rather than leave it. London and the mannered intellectual circles her parents moved in had slowly bred in Mary Reader a feeling which, at its strongest, she could only describe as terror. On her thirtieth birthday, she bought herself a cottage in Hentswell and left her parents to their own contentment.

Once settled on her own, she felt suddenly alive and energetic. In London, her parents had used her, she always thought, much as they used things that happened to be at hand – a bell pull, a cushion, a snuff box. They gave her a kind of grudging attention, became irritated when she got in the way and never bothered to conceal their disappointment that she wasn't more clever and more attractive than she was. But now, mistress of her own small sitting room, going out wherever and whenever she pleased, Mary Reader discovered in herself a desire to communicate with the people in whose midst she now lived, to establish herself in this new community. So she went to church, she joined the Women's Institute, she became a member of the Fête Committee, she wrote a couple of poems for the parish magazine.

By the time war began, most people in Hentswell (which she learned to pronounce Ens'l as all its occupants did) knew her by sight or by hearsay and most of them thought her 'odd'. Mrs Dart, on whom she was a regular caller, told her friends that Miss Reader never seemed to realize that 'you've not got all day to waste, have you?' but said that she thought her neighbourly, 'which is more than you can say for some'. The vicar's wife thought her 'gifted', the shopkeepers found her very polite, and the Misses Groves from across the road thought her cottage delightful. Up at the big house, Madge and the Colonel barely knew of her existence. Until the morning, a blustery November morning, that she pedalled up their drive on her bicycle and rang their doorbell.

It was one of the rare occasions that Madge and the Colonel breakfasted together. Madge was glancing at her *Daily Mail* and the Colonel was reading his *Times*. Sadler had served them and gone back to the kitchen where Vera was making him his third cup of tea of the morning.

'Flamin' front door,' said Vera, cocking her head towards the passage. Sadler had taken off his jacket and Vera picked it up for him.''Ere.'

He put it on, told Vera to keep his tea warm.

Sadler knew Miss Reader by sight. He'd seen her in the village and once in the Public Library in Norwich where he went once a week to change Madge's book. But he was surprised to see her standing at the door. People seldom called on the Bassetts uninvited.

'Good morning. You're wondering what on earth I've come about, I expect!'

She talked, Sadler noticed, as if there were exclamation marks after everything she said.

'I'm sorry to call early! I expect everyone's having breakfast, aren't they?'

'May I say who it is?'

'Oh yes. Mary Reader. Miss Reader!'

'Yes?' Sadler waited, as he had been taught, for her to state her business.

'Well! Are they in? Colonel and Mrs Bassett? I'd like to see them both really. I'm a billeting officer.'

'Will you come in?'

She was wearing an old blue Burberry. It might have been a uniform. And galoshes. It was a cold, rainy morning so she was wearing galoshes.

'Oh your hall,' she said as she stepped in, 'what a wonderful floor! I should have come in the back door with my muddy boots. I must take them off. I'd hate to spoil your lovely floor!'

Sadler took them from her and showed her into the drawing room. Then he put the galoshes in the cloakroom to dry off and went and knocked at the dining room door.

'Come in.' The Colonel's voice always sounded particularly gruff from behind *The Times*.

Sadler went in, opening the door almost noiselessly and shutting it noiselessly behind him.

'Excuse me, Madam, there's a Miss Reader at the door. She'd like a word with you both, at your convenience.'

'Who the hell's Miss Reader, Madge?'

'I've no idea, Geoffrey.'

'You must've. She must be one of your Bridge group.'

'What does she want, Sadler?'

'She's our local billeting officer, Madam.'

'Oh lord! Here it comes, then. You were quite right, Madge.'

'Show her in here, Sadler, will you? Anyone who calls this early can watch us eating. And bring some more coffee for her.'

'Very good, Madam.'

Sadler found Miss Reader examining the pictures in the drawing room.

'I hope they don't mind my looking. I'm a terrible one for nosing!'

'Will you go into the dining room?'

'The dining room? Oh yes, of course. I realized as I came up the drive. You're much too early, I said, you're bound to be disturbing their breakfast.'

'Can I take your mackintosh?'

'Oh yes, thank you. Thank you very much.'

She smiled at Sadler as she unbuttoned it, and he wondered why. Nervousness, no doubt, because her hands were shaking and she seemed to be very hot.

'Follow me, will you?'

He showed her in, saw the Colonel get up, still holding his newspaper and Madge put down her *Mail* and take off her reading glasses.

'Come in, come in,' said the Colonel, 'sit down, will you?'

Sadler shut the door quietly once again and went back to Vera.

'What's the matter with them? ' Vera said when he asked her for more coffee, 'they been 'avin' a piss up?'

Mary Reader sat down. She looked from Madge's face to the Colonel's, both observing her sternly, and felt faint-hearted. She knew that, once she had introduced herself, she'd have to come straight to the point. She would have liked to seize on something in the room, a picture or a bit of furniture – things she knew something about – and talk about it for a while, letting her body settle down, allowing herself time for the right words to come into her head. But they were waiting. They wanted her to say what she had to as quickly as she could, say it and be gone. She dreaded starting because she knew each bit of speech would be punctuated by this nervous laugh of hers that irritated everyone who heard it. She wished she had never learnt to laugh.

'I'm one of the billeting officers for this district . . .' she began.

'I see,' said Madge.

'You've heard on the wireless, I expect – and in the papers – children are being sent out of London.'

'Yes.'

'It's a nightmare for the authorities, as you can

imagine!'

'Yes, I suppose it is.'

'It's quite beyond me how they cope at all; trains and schedules, you know! And of course, so many of the children are unaccompanied.'

'Well, I'd heard that, but I do find it hard to understand,' said Madge. 'I mean, you'd have thought – for young children – the mothers would go with them.'

'Well, you see it's impossible for many of them. I expect you've heard – on the wireless – it's mostly children from the East End, the vulnerable industrial end and the docks, you know. And of course the mothers are working.'

'Oh I see. Yes. Well, I suppose it is difficult for them.'

'So that's where I – we – come in. It's our job to find homes for the ones who are being sent. The reason . . .'

'Well, I know,' interrupted Madge, 'I mean, I imagine that's why you've called, isn't it? To ask us to take in a family? But I think I should explain that the Colonel and I have never had any children ourselves and so we don't know anything at all about looking after them. Not the first thing, do we dear?'

The Colonel was embarrassed. He began digging into his hairy ear with his little finger.

'No, no. I'm afraid we don't.'

'No, do forgive me,' Miss Reader went on. 'I didn't want to sound as if I was *ordering* you. We never approach people like that. There's nothing obligatory at all. It's just that I believe everybody should be approached, you see. Everybody! I don't want to sound naive, but I'd like to put it very simply . . .'

Miss Reader was recovering now and her determination began to return.

'You see, it's *everybody's* war. That's what I believe. And in the circumstances it seems only right that all the burdens should be shared. It's a very naive view, isn't it? I mean of course we can't all join the Expeditionary Force or become Florence Nightingales. Of course we can't. But we can do something to help, all of us, can't we?'

She paused, but the Colonel and Madge just looked at her in silence.

'Quite a few people in Ens'l have helped us out,' she went on, 'in fact we've been amazed by people living in quite straitened circumstances themselves opening their doors – a woman with five of her own taking in two more, that kind of thing. And it just seemed only right to ask you . . . because there's so much *room* here, isn't there? I discussed it with my colleagues of course and they agreed that it was only fair to ask you, to give you the chance . . .'

'Yes. Yes, of course,' said Madge, 'but as I explained, we . . . well, we don't know about children, do we, Geoffrey? We've never had the experience, you see.'

'No, no. Don't misunderstand me. Of course, knowing your circumstances as I do now, I wouldn't dream of burdening you, not with a young family – it simply wouldn't be fair. But you know it's often the older ones – only children, that sort of thing – that are the most difficult to place. Quite a few of the younger mothers will take on children the same age as their own, but it's the older ones, the elevens, twelves and thirteens that are very hard to accommodate. Boys especially, though some are taken on by the farmers; unpaid labour, really! But most mothers choose girls. Less trouble, I suppose, and helpful in the house.'

Miss Reader waited once more for one of them to speak, but they still sat there watching her silently.

'Well,' she said, 'I won't take up any more of your time! I would just say that I'd be very grateful if you'd give it some thought. Just think it over and talk about it and I'll come and see you again, if I may. Next week? It's a *paradise* here, isn't it? A real paradise! You'd be giving a child such a marvellous experience, I'm sure . . .'

She got up. Madge smiled at her.

'Won't you have some coffee?'

'Coffee? Oh no thank you. You will think about it, won't you?'

'Yes, we will,' Madge said.

'We're expecting new arrivals next Thursday or Friday. We don't know how many yet, but we do know that *every* home that is offered will be welcome.'

'Yes, I see.'

'Well . . .'

'Shall I ring for Sadler, Madge?'

'Yes, Geoffrey. Good bye Miss . . . er . . .'

'Reader. Yes. Miss Reader. Goodbye.'

They heard her talking to Sadler in the hall. They sat in silence looking at each other until they heard the front door close behind her. Madge sighed.

'Oh dear, Geoffrey. Doesn't it make your heart sink? Children. Spoiling the house, waking one up at night. We're too old . . .'

'We've no obligation, Madge.'

'Yes, I know that's what she said. But haven't you seen that type before? They never give up.'

'We needn't let her in.'

'Oh don't be silly, Geoffrey. One can't do that. Anyway, maybe she's right, it is everybody's war.'

The next morning, Madge woke feeling very tired. She'd lain awake until it was light, wondering what it might do to her, a noisy, clumsy, probably dirty child, someone else's child in her home, looking to her for care, even for love. I've none to give, she thought. No love, none at all. She resented being asked for it, always had done, except by Geoffrey and his demands were so very reasonable. She believed a child in her house would bring her intense unhappiness, make her tired and old and sour with hatred and guilt. And yet she had thought, lying there, one minute hot, the next cold all through the night, she had thought what a selfish thing I've become. To the

68

women who are sending husbands or sons to die, what a small favour this would seem. A home for one homeless child. Nothing more. Just a home. And not even money to worry about. All the money I want. Thousands and thousands of pounds.

It was a relief when morning came and the shapes in her room began to swim out of the darkness and the birds in her garden started their chirping. The familiarity of her room and the precious knowledge that her garden still separated her from the shifting world outside lulled her and she slept. But on waking an hour or two later, the first thing she thought about was the child. Why me? she asked herself. There must be so many women like me who have been left alone. Why did they come to trouble me?

Madge sat up and brushed her hair. Her eyes smarted and the lids were puffy from lack of sleep. 'Ugly old woman,' she said to her face in the mirror held up to it. But with a bit of rouge on, from the little flat pot she kept on the bedside table, she felt better and rang the bell for Sadler.

He arrived almost at once, setting her tray down carefully on the bed and crossing to the windows to draw the curtains.

'Before you go, Sadler,' Madge said on impulse, 'I'd like to tell you about something that happened yesterday. I'd like to know what you think about it.'

'Yes, Madam?'

'You remember that woman who called while we were having breakfast? You spoke to her, didn't you?'

'She . . . informed me what she'd come about.'

'What do you think, Sadler? I mean, do you think we should?'

Sadler was surprised by her question. He hadn't known her long, but on more than one occasion he'd heard her say she felt uncomfortable – that was the word she'd used – uncomfortable with children. That she was still in doubt about her answer was odd. Even Miss Reader hadn't been hopeful. 'If you could only persuade them,' she'd said to him, 'it's such a paradise here. You couldn't give any child a more precious gift.'

Sadler had believed the matter closed and wondered only what they would do if the Government's plea became an order.

'It's so difficult, you see,' Madge went on, 'to know what's expected of one at a time like this. Don't you agree?'

'It is, yes.'

'But you don't think that at all really, do you? Of course you don't. You think the Colonel and I should agree to take in a child, don't you?'

Sadler was about to lie, but she cut him off.

'And of course you're right. I know you're right. Why shouldn't we share our home? Give someone's boy or girl some nice memories. But would they be nice, Sadler? You see, we've never been close to any children, the Colonel and I. We've never had to handle them. We don't understand children, only insofar as we were children once – I think. But it's not enough, is it? I mean, the countless things one has to think up just to amuse them. All that, day after day . . . and we're getting on, you know . . . we really are . . .'

She was quite distressed. Sadler waited a second or two before he spoke.

'If you like,' he said quietly, 'if you thought it was my place, I could take responsibility. There were kiddies at my last job, the one in Scarborough. They were left on their own a lot and they used to come to me for games, to have a laugh. I learnt a lot about kiddies there.'

Madge frowned.

'Really, Sadler? Did you? Could you, I mean?'

'I'd be glad to try.'

And now she smiled. Because that might be different.

That might alter the whole thing and make it bearable. If the child stayed in the servants' hall, had its meals there, the kind of meals it'd be used to, she'd be glad to spend some of her time with it, take it shopping or for walks round the garden. Her conscience would be clear because she'd be paying for it all, and who knew if, under these conditions, she might not come to like the child.

'It seems an awful lot to ask of you, Sadler.'

'No. I'd be glad.'

'We'd be on hand, of course, if anything went wrong.'

'Oh yes.'

'And money, naturally. We'd see you had everything that was needed.'

'Oh I doubt one extra would cost a lot.'

'But extra for you, of course, if you're going to do two jobs . . .'

Sadler had saved her. When she'd finished her breakfast and the tray had been taken away, she turned her head from the light and slept an untroubled sleep till lunchtime.

The big house with its tended garden, its woods and its orchard, had stayed in Miss Reader's mind as she looked out on Mrs Dart's patch of scuffed grass. It stayed with her as she went round Hentswell from door to door and saw the cramped rooms where many of the new 'vacuees' would live. And by the end of the week, her determination had grown: she would place a child in the Colonel's care or count herself a failure in the job she had taken on.

She was surprised to be greeted with a smile when she turned up at the house. Madge herself came out into the porch as she arrived and led her into the drawing room, where a fire was blazing.

'I'm so glad you've come back, Miss . . .'

'Reader.'

71

'Miss Reader. You see, we did need time to think this over. I imagine everyone does, don't they? But I didn't want you to get the impression that we were set against it. I feel I must have given you that impression, didn't I, when we last met? But as I explained to you, I – we've – never had children of our own, and coming out of the blue like that . . . But we've had time now to think it over and we do feel that you were quite right, it is everybody's war and I wouldn't like anyone to accuse us of not doing our bit. The only thing that I've been wondering about is the *procedure* – you know. I mean, does one simply sit here and wait for one or does one go and . . . choose one?'

Miss Reader told Madge to go down to the Reception Centre in the church hall early on Friday morning. The evacuee train was due in at nine and it was a question of first come first served, rather along the lines of a livestock auction, except that you didn't pay – the Government paid you, eight and six a week for a girl and ten shillings for a boy. The children would be wearing labels with their names and addresses on; it was just a question of picking the one you wanted.

Madge was relieved. It had been decided of course that the child would sleep upstairs in one of the servants' rooms and have meals with Sadler and Vera, but still, it was nice to know she'd be able to choose the face she'd see from her window, a face she'd have to meet from time to time.

'It sounds a very sensible arrangement,' she told Miss Reader. 'We'll be there.'

'We' meant Madge and Sadler. The Colonel stayed at home, treasuring perhaps his last few hours of peace. He sat in his study, listening to the wireless, and the news announcer told him that still no bombs had fallen on London and that there were 'disturbing signs' that many of the families evacuated from the East End had failed to adapt to the country wastes and were trickling home. The news reassured him. The unwelcome intrusion into his quiet life might soon be gone.

The train came in. It was only a short walk from Hentswell station, but the children, herded along by volunteer chaperones, began to run. The long hours spent in the stuffy, crowded train had snuffed out any excitement they might have felt and had left them thirsty and tired. The promise of a beaker of orangeade as they left the station was enough to send them scuttling down the village street, shouting and jumping, some laughing at long last and others crying as they were pulled along. Their homes vanished now as their new surroundings pressed in on them, but they were too bewildered to know what to make of them, too thirsty to do anything but keep running. The mothers, the few that had come, were forced to run, too, pulled along by their children.

'Don't run, stop running!' they shouted, hating this embarrassing, disorderly progress.

As they passed, the silent, safe community of Hentswell received them with little titters of laughter.

Once inside the church hall, the children jostled for the orangeade laid out on long trestle tables, and the mothers hung back, aware of the group of people sitting to one side and looking them up and down. Miss Reader and the vicar's wife came forward: there was a cup of tea for the mothers, if they liked, and then perhaps, they'd like to collect their children and wait in family groups. They drank the tea, glad of that at least. But time was casting them adrift and they looked about them in blank misery. They felt like beggars.

'Go on, Sadler,' said Madge.

Her eye had singled out a pale, fair boy, standing on his own, holding his beaker of orangeade, but not drinking it, staring in awe at the strangers come to meet him.

He was remembering what his Ma had said before he

73

left: 'Don't look so bleedin' miserable, Tom, or no one'll choose you. For Gawd's sake smile, can't yer?' He couldn't. He hadn't known till the evening before that he was going. No one had told him. And he'd stayed awake all night, frightened to go to sleep in case they put him on the train before he'd said goodbye. Then the morning had come and a coach had arrived to collect him, and his Ma in her dressing gown, shivering in the early morning cold, hadn't even hugged him, just held his shoulders and kissed his forehead and told him to hurry up.

'He looks a nice quiet one,' Madge said. 'Go and talk to him, Sadler.'

'Sadler crossed the room to where the boy stood.

'Hello, lad,' Sadler said, smiling. 'What's your name, son?'

The boy fingered the top button of his coat.

'It's on the label, mister.'

Tom called everyone 'mister'. Except Madge, whom he never addressed at all, and Vera, whom he liked and called 'auntie'. The Colonel, of course, would have preferred to be called 'Colonel' or 'Sir'. 'You should call me "Colonel",' he told Tom, 'or "Sir".' But Tom was confused. The only people he'd ever addressed as 'Sir' were his schoolteachers, and in his history books Colonels only popped up when there was a war going on and they had to go off and command. They never seemed to have homes, let alone stay in them, when everyone else was outside fighting. To Tom, this argued that Colonel Bassett couldn't be a real Colonel. He thought of asking Vera, but as far as he could see, Vera and the Colonel had never met, so he doubted that she knew anything about it. Only much later did he think to ask Sadler and Sadler told him that the Colonel was 'retired' – a word Tom believed meant some kind of incurable illness. After that, he did call

74

the Colonel 'Colonel' when he remembered, mostly out of pity.

Tom's first comment about the house as they drove up – Madge and Wren in front, Tom and Sadler behind – was that it looked like Buckingham Palace.

Madge, feeling light-hearted now that it was 'all over', said: 'I'm afraid you won't find the King here, dear.' And Tom said flatly: 'No. I know. The King's in London. My Ma said she thought 'e was quite brave to stay there.'

'Oh I agree,' said Madge, 'I agree with your Ma.'

The car and his empty stomach had made Tom feel sick. His face was as white as chalk as they led him up the stone steps and into the great, dark hall. Looking at him, Sadler could imagine the nightmare he was going through, so he took his hand, anxious to spare him any further meetings and told Madge that he thought it best if Tom went straight to the kitchen and had a warm drink and something to eat. Madge agreed. Best to get it sorted out right from the start, she thought, he's Sadler's responsibility.

When Vera greeted him with her 'come on in, duck,' sat him down at the scrubbed table with a mug of tea and told him she'd fry him a couple of sausages, he felt better.

'Ta,' he said.

''Ad an awful journey then, love?' she asked him.

'They didn't give us no drinks,' said Tom, clasping his tea.

His eyes followed her as she moved around the kitchen. All the women he'd ever met – until today – had been a bit like Vera. Fatter or thinner, with different hair, different aprons, but like her in essence. Even his Ma, though younger, had a manner something like Vera's. He hoped he could just stay there in the warm kitchen, watching her.

Sadler was watching him. He was a thin boy and quite small for what, judging from his face, his age appeared to be. His eyes were a washed-out blue, large in a bony face,

75

and they looked steadily and carefully at things. He was still wearing his coat, too short in the sleeves, and with the label on it.

'You warm enough, Tom?' Sadler asked.

'Yes,' said Tom.

'Like to take your coat off?'

'Yes.'

Tom put down his tea reluctantly, then stood up and unbuttoned his coat. Sadler took it from him, reading the label as he hung it up: *Tom Trent, 68 Woodbridge Buildings, Coston Lane, London. E.5. Aged 11 years.*

'When's your birthday, Tom?' Sadler asked him.

'Nineteenth of March, mister.'

'Well, that's funny – day after mine.'

Tom grinned at last.

'How old are you, mister?'

'Same age as the year. You didn't know that, did you, Vera?'

'Lor no, Mr Sadler,' she teased, 'I always thought you was older than me.' Then to Tom: 'Certainly looks it, don't 'e?'

But Tom was looking away.

'My Ma's thirty-one,' he said.

It was this business of Tom's Ma, the way, during his first weeks at the house, each conversation ended with some reference to her, that made Sadler want to care for Tom. Trying to remember what it was like to be eleven, Sadler decided that had he been separated from Annie at that age, he would have wanted to die. So close to her had he stayed, so absolutely necessary to his life had her almost constant presence become, that even one night away from her would have been torment. And if – for whatever reason – she'd sent him away, as Tom's mother had done, he knew he would have resisted all communication with the strangers who replaced her and withdrawn into total silence. Sadler thought he saw in Tom something of what he himself had been, would make this the excuse for loving him.

But he was mistaken. Tom was nothing like Jack Sadler had been. Despite the careful ways in which the boy kept stating apparently random bits of information about his Ma so that no one would forget that he belonged to her, he had long been forced into an unwilling independence from her. She'd come and gone. Gone, often, by the time he kicked his way home from school. *Don't go out*, notes on the kitchen table had read, *Sausage roll for your tea*. He always stayed up waiting for her, reading his *Champion*, had fallen asleep sometimes, till she woke him up putting the light on.

'Aunties' replaced her. Once or twice a Nigerian woman from the flat next door called Martha-Ann brought him round a great spicy bowl of something or other for his supper, and laughed and clapped her podgy hands while he gulped it down. He liked Martha-Ann. They would play noughts and crosses on a slate and he could beat her. Or listen to the wireless. He wasn't allowed to touch the wireless if no grown ups were there, but Martha-Ann always turned it on for him and at that time in the evening there was usually a funny show that they enjoyed; and Martha-Ann would laugh at all the jokes.

Tom's Ma – so different from Annie Sadler – couldn't bear to do any fussing and petting over her kid, it didn't seem natural to her. Tom had never been hugged much, or had her attention for longer than was necessary to keep him quiet. Tom loved her because she was his Ma. He was glad when she stayed in and talked to him. But he had also come to realize that as Mas went, she wasn't all that good. Martha-Ann's children were often picked up and given wet kisses and taken to the funfair on Saturdays. They even had a sweet tin on the window sill with lemon sherberts in it, and on Sundays they sat down to huge dinners that had taken all morning to cook. Tom once said to Martha-Ann that he wished she was his Ma, but the remark brought instant disaster. He immediately felt ashamed of having 'betrayed' his own Ma, and Martha-Ann started shedding a great Niagara of tears.

When the war had started and people said the Germans would drop bombs on the East End, Tom's Ma thought it best to heed the Government's warning and send Tom away. She told herself that this would be 'best all round'. Tom would have a nice time in the country and, bombs or no, at thirty-one she would at last have regained her freedom. When the bus left, taking the boy away, she made herself a cup of tea and lit a cigarette, feeling happier than she had done for years.

For his part, Tom experienced a very real despair as the bus turned out of his street. It wasn't leaving that was so bad, it was the feeling of having failed.

It was some weeks before Sadler could piece together enough of what Tom had told him to be able to follow the muddled turnings the boy's life had taken. But on that first evening, climbing the stairs to the top landing with Tom, Sadler racked his brain for something to say, some promise, he thought, some word to reassure the child that he could give him – what? Friendship? He supposed that was it: friendship. But Sadler had never really understood the term. He'd either loved people, or been indifferent to them. Understanding, then? But understanding was so close to pity and children recognized pity for the base emotion Sadler knew it to be. So keep quiet, he told himself, say nothing. Instead, he took Tom's hand as they went into his little room.

'You be all right, then?' Sadler asked him.

'I'm OK, mister,' Tom said.

Sadler drew his curtains and left him to himself. Tom sat down on the bed, took a dirty rubber out of one of his pockets and started rubbing his knee.

Miss Reader called after a week. She made a point, she said, of going round all the evacuee foster homes as often as she could, to find out how things were going. Clothes, she explained, had turned out to be one of the biggest problems. The long summer was to blame. The weather had been so hot in the south of England that many of the London children had been sent off wearing sandals and cotton blouses. And now, of course, it was beginning to turn cold, and some of them didn't even possess a warm coat. The Government was to blame in part, Miss Reader stressed, so little warning was given that many of the mothers panicked and forgot to pack properly, just sent the youngsters off with what they had to hand.

'Oh Tom has a coat,' Madge assured her, anxious for Miss Reader to be gone. 'Anyway, if he needs clothes and things, you can be sure we'll get them for him.'

'Good,' said Miss Reader. 'Now what about bed wetting? Have you had any trouble?'

'Oh good heavens no! I don't think so. I don't make the beds, you understand, but I'm sure Jane or Betty would have reported anything like that.'

'You would be sure not to scold, if it does happen, wouldn't you? It's the strange surroundings, you see. They get over it in time, when they get used to you.'

'I see. One can't help feeling sorry . . . It must be. . . I don't know . . . terrible, I suppose.'

'It's a social upheaval quite unparalleled in recent years. But at least we know they're safe, don't we?'

'I don't expect anyone knows how long it'll last, do they?'

'Months – or years. Our lives will change, maybe for the better.'

Madge couldn't imagine a 'better'. Money had bought her such treasures and when she moved among them she believed she was perfectly happy. There was Geoffrey, of course, so much less bright than all those shiny medals he'd won at Gallipoli, and a bit disorientated these last years, with no orders to give. He'd taken to making inventories: inventories of his library of military history, inventories of everything in the house worth more than a hundred pounds, inventories of the things he kept in his bedroom cupboards – stud boxes, button shiners, clothes brushes, shoe horns, cigar cases, innumerable ties and pairs of cufflinks, and his medals. Gives me something to do, he explained. And Madge thought he's probably a bit batty by now – perhaps we both are. But Geoffrey loved her. Geoffrey had cherished her all these years, without asking for much in return. She hated to think of a life without him.

'Don't you agree?' Miss Reader asked.

'What did you say?'

'Don't you agree that change can be for the better? Take the last war.'

'Oh,' said Madge, 'we were still quite young then. It makes all the difference, doesn't it?'

Miss Reader abandoned the conversation. Madge told her that she'd find Tom in the garden, if she wanted to see him. Out at the back, Madge thought, or down at the stream.

'He seems to like the stream,' she said.

Miss Reader went out and made rather ungainly progress through the damp orchard grass. She had caught sight of Sadler standing on the bank of the stream and welcomed the chance to talk to him again. Because he puzzled her. Behind the butler's convention of playing deaf, she judged him to be an intelligent observer. He himself seemed to invite observation. He looked, not down, when he spoke to you, but right at you and Miss Reader liked that look.

Tom was down in the stream. He'd collected as many large stones as he could find and was trying to make a dam. But the current was stronger than it seemed; he could hardly get two or three stones together before the water parted them and sent them scudding into the bank. Sadler was watching him, biting on a pipe that had gone out.

'It's no good, Tom,' he was saying, 'we'll have to go and look for some bigger stones.'

'There ain't none any bigger.'

'Or use something else as a foundation, a log or something.'

'Yeah, OK.'

Miss Reader waved to them.

'Hullo there!'

Sadler turned and Tom looked up. Miss Reader sensed that they resented the intrusion.

'What a lovely stream, isn't it?' she said.

'Wot she want?' Tom asked Sadler.

'Oh, I've come to see if everything's all right. You remember me, don't you, Tom? I was at the Centre when you all arrived.'

'I don't remember you.'

'We're OK though, aren't we Tom?' Sadler cut in quickly.

'I dunno.'

Tom climbed up the farther bank of the stream and began to wander off. Miss Reader turned to Sadler.

'He's with you most of the time, is he?'

Sadler's eyes were following Tom.

'Yes.'

'I suppose everyone's happy with the arrangement?'

'Oh yes.'

'Of course, it's very wrong of them . . .'

'My choice, Miss.'

'Oh I see.'

Sadler called out: 'Don't get lost, Tom!' But the boy didn't turn. Just kept walking in his aimless fashion.

'Well . . .'

81

Miss Reader would have liked to talk to Sadler. She felt like telling him not to bother with all that politeness, not with her. She might belong by birth to the class it flattered, but she only recognized its superfluousness. What hope for understanding can there possibly be, she felt like saying to him, if all we can say is what's expected of us, the things charted and set down? But it was coming out with questions of that sort that had so often landed her in trouble at her father's dinner table with everyone looking at her in astonishment and her mother asking: 'Is this another of your Equality things, Mary?'

She felt suddenly miserable, thinking to herself how nice – how *right* really – it would have been to take Sadler's arm and walk gently along, comfortable as she walked, with her arm tucked in like that, and just talk. She was so conscious of the weight of her loneliness. It would have been a blessed relief to have rested it, if only for a while, on him.

'Well . . .' she said again.

She followed Sadler's gaze and saw that Tom was almost out of sight now, gone right across the big meadow. Sadler took his pipe out of his mouth and knocked it against the tree. Then he turned and looked at Miss Reader.

'He's best left alone, I think. For a while yet, anyway.'

'Tom?'

'He keeps most things inside him. Never even answers a question straight.'

Miss Reader assumed her professional voice.

'What does he talk about?'

'The things he reads. And his Ma.'

Sadler was disappointed. He'd told Tom that he'd spend this, his day off, with him. He'd even suggested he pack them up some sandwiches, go for a long walk, watch them burning off stubble, maybe even go as far as the river and have a picnic there. He'd been looking forward to it.

Now he turned his back on the stream and started to walk towards the house.

Miss Reader followed.

'I was just thinking, Mr Sadler, if you do find the days a bit long . . . thinking up things for him to do, you know . . . I live in the village and you could bring him down one afternoon, perhaps on your day off, for a cup of tea?'

'Thank you, Miss,' Sadler said, 'but I wouldn't like to put you to the trouble.'

'Oh, it wouldn't be any trouble.'

'And as I said, he's best left alone . . .'

'Oh, of course, just at the moment. Period of adjustment – that's what they call it, don't they? But in a week or two.'

'Thank you, Miss,' said Sadler. Then he nodded goodbye and walked quickly away from her towards the back door.

IV

Sadler was aware of the spring. When you got old, or so he found, all that spring did to you was remind you of other springs, springs that had bloomed into summers and burned out long ago, springs when the sight of straight, bright grass coming up in last winter's pale hay had been enough to set your mind muddling forward to some new endeavour, springs when you weren't old.

He couldn't remember when spring had started to hurt him. Ages ago, probably. He'd been old it seemed for so long. Old at fifty, and since then a shameful decline. Looking at the buds, the contained, strong growth everywhere creeping out, he tried to imagine his body crushed and crammed into one of those tiny sheaths, reduced to something no bigger than a bean, but with the whole of its existence in front, not behind, the whole of his being curled there, growing, the flower and the leaf yet to come. He spat. Silly old fool, what thoughts!

But this happened quite a lot now, particularly on days when he was tired. He'd have these odd notions about himself, shunting his mind backwards in time, dwelling on things that once seemed important and on things that had never happened. A muddle, he decided. That's all I've become. Not coherent any more, even. Typical case of senile decay. Decay of body into lumbering old wreck, decay of mental faculties.

He leant on his stick looking at his orchard. So foolish to drag what little power of thinking left to me backwards. Why not think forward into the tiny bit – moments even? – left to come? And try to understand. Understand yourself at least. Because what's there in the past to give you any clue? What's to show for all that time? An awareness of your mediocrity, a growing despondency. That was all. Nothing else of any note, was there? After seventy-six years – from soft-skinned child grubbing on a green square to a blotchy old man who limped, and whose mouth, for some humiliating reason, made too much saliva – was that all he could think of to say? He searched, of course. The search had become frenzied. Now hardly an hour went by without him finding some buried splinter of his existence and picking at it. But, probe as he did, he could find nothing much of any significance: just the odd day – odd *hour*, really, because that was the burning time of the fuses occasionally lit with happiness – yes, the odd hour of wonder. There were, he decided, about seven or eight of these in all that time. A long time, though, or just a few minutes? Impossible to tell how long, like the dreams he'd had, or like the film, one of the few he'd ever seen, where they'd gone through three generations in as many hours and Elizabeth Taylor had grown old and died as he sat there going through a bag of popcorn.

And now the spring had turned up again. Still half immersed, but there. There. Even in the sounds he could hear. There. To taunt him, he supposed. And why not? A foolish spectacle, he was, leaning on his stick – like the beggar in fairy tales who pops out of a wood and alters the whole story. No story left for him to alter. The ending was already set down.

When? He often thought there must be a point when there was still a choice to be made, or was it made before he was born? By the mother he'd loved or the father he'd never seen? Or was Greg Sadler to blame, for dying?

* * *

Greg Sadler's death made Annie a prisoner. Her future, from that point, was determined not by her own wishes but by her need for money. She found no alternative but to gather up her child and move reluctantly forwards to the only thing that offered – a position as chamber-maid at Milord's house.

They gave her a narrow room, furnished with a brass bed, a chair, a chest of drawers and a child's picture. They gave her food and a uniform and a few shillings a week. They gave her milk for Jack. On her days off, she'd go to see Betsy who'd given up her job at Mrs Collard's and was getting married that Easter to one John Thomas, assistant manager of the pork pie factory.

Betsy was too delighted with herself to want to muddy her hands in Annie's sorrows. She told herself that by communicating to Annie all her joy ('just *think*, Annie, go to Mrs Collard's, he said, and choose whatever you like, *whatever material you like* for your dress') she'd brighten her drab day. 'And in a few years, or so he says, he's certain to be manager – imagine, manager at thirty-two – and then we'll be really set up, won't we?' Because Annie had always been able to be happy about other people's good fortune, hadn't she? And what was there to say about Annie's life now?

The work wasn't so hard that it calloused her hands or rubbed the skin off her knees. Miss Rhodes, the house-keeper, took a fancy to her and gave her sweets for little Jack. And Milady, when she saw her, usually smiled. Merely, she had lost her freedom. 'But there's no sense in moaning, Annie, is there?' said Betsy, giving her friend's bondage her reluctant attention. 'I mean, if you think about it another way, you were lucky to be taken on at all with the baby and that and it was really only because of my Dad knowing that Mr Knightley . . .'

Her day began at five. So comfortable, so far off, they seemed, those mornings when she'd tiptoed down at seven to light the fire and make breakfast for her father. Now she fumbled in the near darkness, waking Jack who slept at her side, dressing him, telling him each morning not to make a sound till they were downstairs. Then making a porridge for them both, something warm before she began work laying fires, with Jack traipsing round after her. The 'stick man' she called him, because she knew she had to make fun of the work, giving him the basket of kindling to carry. That early, it was very cold in the enormous house. It would have been wonderful, Annie often thought, to put a match to the fires she laid. Then, cleaning the brass stair rods, Jack with a soft rag following – the 'shiny man' now. But they had to hurry, be out of the way before Milord came down for his breakfast on the dot of seven. And then came the best moment of the day: they'd go back to the kitchen, warm now with all the stoves burning, and have a mug of tea, and Cook, if she had time, would fry up the bacon rind for Jack and he'd eat it with his fingers.

They let him play in the garden. Not in front of the house where he could be seen by anyone coming up the drive, but out at the back, safely out of sight beyond a little pine wood. Annie would lose sight of him for hours on end, crane out of top windows, trying to catch a glimpse of him now and then as she went about her morning tasks, fearful if she couldn't see him, but 'don't you go chasing after him,' Miss Rhodes had warned, 'you've got a job to do.'

'Well, be thankful they let him play,' Betsy remarked.

Annie grew silent. She talked to Jack when they were on their own, but avoided the servants' hall and angered Miss Rhodes by being 'cold'. She missed the familiar, self-important little town and gradually the great expanses of field and wood that surrounded her became as unfriendly as a high wall. She drifted. Days, cold, quiet, became years.

Jack grew up. He was bought a satchel and sent off to the village school, walking there each day, a mile there and a mile back. It was at this time that Annie began stealing books from the library to read to him. *Ivanhoe* took her a year to get through. There was something about the print and the heaviness of the book, she said, that seemed to make her sleepy. But Jack always looked forward to those reads. Coming home from school, he'd think firstly about his tea – bread and jam and sometimes muffins, if Cook had made any – and then about the next bit of the story, told in that gentle, whispering voice and the nightly ritual of the book being hidden away like some priceless treasure under the mattress. Part of the magic of these stories lay in his own role as conspirator with Annie. 'You must never say a word about it, Jackie. Not to Cook or Miss Rhodes or Mr Knightley or anyone at all. They'd send us away if they found out, and then what would happen?'

But he was old enough, aware enough by that time to have made plans to save them, if that day ever came. The plans changed with the stories, and sometimes, when he'd made a particularly exciting one, he secretly hoped they would be discovered and sent away. Then his hour would come and off they'd set, he buoyant, strong, full of reassurance and his mother mysteriously and suddenly infirm, leaning on his shoulder. 'Oh don't worry,' he said, when she began the thing about not telling, 'I'll look after you.'

Then came a morning when, dressed for school, sitting on the hearthrug with his bag of kindling, watching Annie shovel out the ashes under the drawing room grate, his eyes lighted on the grand piano. Its sides and lid were inlaid with a marvellous pattern of flowers and leaves and it shone. Tired in the early mornings now that he spent his days at school and bored by the ritual of the fire, he left his kindling bag, went over to the piano and opened the lid.

'Jack, don't!'

'Why can't I?'

'Come away, Jackie.'

'Just one note. Let me.'

'No. You'll wake the whole house.'

'I won't.'

'Leave it, Jack.'

'You play, then.'

'No!'

'Please, Ma.'

'No.'

'Just one thing.'

'I can't remember anything.'

'Oh go on.'

Annie was standing by him now, her hand ready to snatch his away.

'Just something. *Please*, Ma.'

It was so long since she'd sat down at a piano. Her own had been sold after Greg died. Her fingers had stiffened since then, but she believed she still knew one or two pieces in her head and, standing looking at the keyboard, she was suddenly curious, suddenly longed to find out if the process would begin and her hands would remember where to go. She hesitated. To know that she could still play would have been so nice. She thought, if she could remember even one piece, she might take out some of the old sheets of music and go through them humming the notes, knowing that if ever she got the chance . . .

'No one'll hear, Ma. They're asleep.'

'Well . . .'

'Something quiet. Couldn't you?'

'We shouldn't.'

'But you always told me you could play.'

Jack got up and she sat down on the stool, automatically adjusting it to the right height and feeling the pedals with her feet. In front of her the notes were surprisingly familiar. She recognized patterns. Jack stood behind her, like someone waiting to turn her music.

Then she started to play. A piece out of her girlhood past, nameless, Chopin she thought, but what key, what number? She couldn't remember. She had the music somewhere. She could look it up and then one day play it again properly with the notes in front of her, all the right notes. But she couldn't get to the end. Somewhere, after a perfectly remembered beginning, the process stopped and her hands were lost.

'Go on,' Jack said.

She was dejected now.

'Can't remember any more, love.'

'Bet you can.'

'No, honest. Anyway, we've got work to do, haven't we?'

Jack walked to school thinking about that scrap of music. At break-time, when they went out into the playground, he told his friend, Eric Lufty, that his mother could play better than Mrs Dean, the music teacher, but Eric Lufty said he didn't think Mrs Dean played very well anyhow. So Jack supposed it must have been *what* she played. It wasn't a march or a hymn or Activity Music like they had at school, it was something else. 'It's better, anyway,' he said.

Then when he got back in the afternoon, going into the kitchen as he always did for his tea, he found no one there. Usually Cook had laid a plate for him and put a loaf out, and his mother, if she wasn't busy, would be making tea. But the kitchen was deserted, its scrubbed floor damp as it always was in the afternoons, but not a soul there.

'Ma!'

But Mr Knightley came out of the servants' hall, his face very straight and hard like it was when he served in the dining room.

'Sit down, Jack.'

Jack took off his satchel and sat at the table.

'Now listen to me.'

90

There was an ominous whispering quality to Mr Knightley's voice as he began.

'I want you to realize, Jack, that it is only through my intervention that your mother wasn't dismissed at once. There'll be no second chance, Jack, and you know quite well what I'm talking about. Servants in this house go into his Lordship's rooms to do their work and once that work is done, they go back to where they belong. They touch nothing. They take nothing.'

Jack's heart began to race as he thought of *Tom Sawyer* under the mattress.

'Do you understand, Jack?'

He was on the point of saying: 'We don't steal them, Mr Knightley. We only borrow them.' And then, just in time, he remembered the endlessly repeated swearing to secrecy and said nothing.

'Do you?'

Dumb, Jack nodded.

'That piano is priceless – a priceless object. I told His Lordship that I was sure your mother never would have dreamed of touching it if you hadn't asked her and all I can tell you, Jack, is that you're very lucky, very lucky indeed to find yourself in the care of such understanding people . . .'

So *Tom Sawyer* was safe after all. It was that little bit of music that worried them.

'Where's my tea, Mr Knightley?'

'I want this lesson learnt, Jack Sadler, so I instructed Cook . . .'

'Aren't I getting any tea?'

'I instructed Cook not to prepare any meal for you this evening. Now go to your room.'

He climbed the stairs, dragging his satchel. In the room, he found his mother sitting by their high window, looking out, down on to the summer garden. She was sitting very, very still. So still that Jack was frightened. He

91

went up to her and clambered on to her knee and put his face down into her shoulder.

She held him for a while, saying nothing, then she said: 'Wouldn't it be nice, Jackie, if we had a rocking chair? Don't you think it would?'

And after that day, she tried not to speak to anyone at all, only to him. He noticed that if they were in the kitchen having breakfast and Mr Knightley came in, she started telling him to hurry up and get off to school, and if Mr Knightley spoke to her, even kindly, she'd answer him with a mumbled word and never look at him.

'I don't like Mr Knightley,' he told her loyally.

'Oh he's all right in his way,' she answered.

But after a while, it seemed to Jack that she hardly noticed other people. She worked with them, ate her meals with them, thanked them if they gave her things for him (sweets usually, but once a book on British Dogs from Miss Rhodes) but seemed to pretend all the time that they weren't there. And, one weekend, Jack was invited to Eric Lufty's house. It was tiny. It was the smallest house Jack had ever been in, but it was all theirs, every room. And Mrs Lufty was a mountain of a mother who talked loudly and cheerfully about anything that came into her head and to anyone who happened to be there. Jack came back feeling small and sorrowful.

'Why don't you talk to people more, Ma?' he asked Annie that night. But all she did was pretend to be asleep. Left him lying there with his eyes wide open, worrying about her, wondering if, in the end, her silences would engulf him too. Because the future seemed to lie shrouded in these great folds of silence. Pointless to invent his dramatic plans for their salvation if this was all there was, this quietness.

Without the familiar pattern of work and sleep through which her body moved, Jack feared that Annie would cease to exist. In his worst imaginings, there was nothing as terrible as that, so he must watch over her constantly and each hour he spent away, wasn't it possible that he deprived her of an hour of life?

Then, without any warning, they sent him away. They were sorry, they told Annie, but they couldn't go on paying out for him past his fourteenth birthday. She must understand. So a position had been found for him. A friend of Milady's wanted an under footman and was quite happy to take him on at once and train him. He'd start on a very small wage, of course, but he was a bright boy and already knew a lot about the way a big house was managed. He'd do well. Milady wouldn't be surprised if he ended up as butler one of these days.

Annie wept. Was it really all those years ago that she'd held him, tiny little thing, in her arms? With Greg standing over and saying: 'You never believe it till it happens, do you? You never believe it till it happens!' Fourteen years, gone in one yesterday.

And Jack? He spent his last days in Milord's house chattering excitedly, telling everyone that next term he'd be in the one from top form at school. But the adult faces looked at him strangely. Pity made them feel uncomfortable and the servants' hall was out of joint until he'd gone.

Summer. High summer, but a rainy one, if Jack remembered rightly. And with the rain must have settled a kind of despair. Thank Christ that particular time was past, then. At least nothing much else in his life had been as bad as that. He'd made strides after that. Got on. Because it occurred to him at that time that it was lack of control over his own life that had brought him to this loneliness. And he decided, shining the buttons on his new uniform, to gain that control.

There was a butler at the new house, a Mr Keynes, who had once been flattered by Madam by saying that she thought him 'a very perceptive man'. So, as if striving perpetually to demonstrate his powers of perception, not only to Madam but to the servants as well, he made constant observations about everything and everyone. After only one week he pronounced about Jack Sadler. 'I'd call him a goer,' he said. But the other servants couldn't agree. Because the boy seemed miserable, a burdensome presence in the household, and they eyed him as a traitor. It was a household with Rules, they tried to make him understand, the most fundamental of which insisted that Servants Look Cheerful At All Times. And it was true that, just as a class of schoolchildren see a longed-for outing snatched away because one of them is deemed unworthy of it, so the servants at Thripton House came under general disfavour if they were not seen to be 'pulling together'.

Madam, conveying displeasure in every one of her tight little movements, would tread and retread the hearthrug in the servants' hall, sprouting angry little phrases as if she were handing out sticks to a line of hands assembled there. She kept going up and down, up and down the line, deciding she hadn't given them enough, up and down, up and down, while they stood silent and still, taking the sticks, watching her bundle of them get smaller and their own begin to grow. Then she'd send them away. She had more, the bundle wasn't gone yet, but they'd have to wait for the rest, come back another day.

'So do you understand, Keynes?'

'Madam.'

'Discontent in the servants' hall . . . I'm relying on you . . . as head of the staff . . . and the others must clearly understand . . . to report anything like that to me . . . at once . . . never to my husband . . . because he mustn't be bothered with petty things . . . to me . . . do you understand?'

'Yes, Madam.'

Then when she'd gone, Keynes waited for the silence to settle before he turned to them all.

'Sadler.'

'Yes, Mr Keynes.'

'I'd like you to pay special attention to what I'm going to say.'

So Jack stood, fiddling with the smart buttons on his jacket, and heard that on no account were any of the staff to let their feelings interfere with the jobs they were paid to do. 'And that means, Sadler . . .' He jerked his head up as his name jumped out at him. '. . . that whatever you might feel about coming here, about us, about your employers, you are from now on to show us that you can behave as a pleasant human being. I have no quarrel, none at all, with the way you do your work. I would go so far as to say that you do most things very carefully and well. But you must hold your head up, Sadler. Hold your head up!'

The others were all looking at him. Confusion mounted inside him, squeezing his breath, burning his cheeks, till it welled out of him. Tears. Keynes cleared his throat. Someone, one of the young housemaids, put an arm round his shoulder.

'Cheer up, love. No one's hurting you.'

But they were. The next day he had a letter from his mother. 'Oh, Jackie,' it said, 'I put *The Mill on the Floss* back on the shelf today. We never got to the end, did we? It wasn't one of your favourites, I know, especially after I told you George Eliot was a girl, but we always had a rule, remember, to finish the ones we started . . .' No anger in her letter, just resignation – 'I put *The Mill on the Floss* back on the shelf.' So you see, she seemed to be saying, you feel things much less, in fact you hardly feel them at all, if you don't let yourself be angry. And things improve. The maids, for instance, they, neat as pigeons in their grey dresses and white collars, singled him out for their maternal affection after that talking-to. Mary, the fattest of the pigeons, smuggled out titbits to him, picked from the dishes sent back from the dining room, and took to giving him this little peck of a kiss on the top of his head. So he grew to like Mary, fat, talkative Mary, the antithesis of Annie Sadler.

There was a lot of chores to be done. Walking all day long, up and down and backwards and forwards through the rambling house, fetching and carrying logs and coal and milk churns and sacks of potatoes and other things that were heavy and made him go slowly; sometimes just a message in his head and then he ran, as fast as he could, so that he wouldn't have time to forget it. His favourite job was cleaning shoes. They were all lined up for him, early each morning, on a table under a very bright electric light bulb in the cellar. It was his first job of the day and he did it with faultless care. And Madam's shoes, all different colours, with tall, square heels and little spaces at the end for the toe to peep through, he marvelled at them. Because not only were they incredibly shaped, sprouting soft little straps and little buds of buttons, but they never seemed to *need* cleaning. Day after day they came down to him and he tried always to make them shine more, but months passed and they were still perfect, still hardly worn.

'Madam,' Keynes told him, 'says you clean her shoes very nicely. So keep it up, keep up a high standard in everything you do and we shall all be pleased to see you get on.' Then he added: 'And I'll give you a tip, Sadler. If you want to make friends in this life, always tell others the good that's said about them and think very carefully before passing on the bad.' And two things occurred to Sadler: first that Mr Keynes looked at him strangely, and secondly that his mother never thought, let alone said, anything critical or unkind about anyone and yet she had no friends, only Aunt Betsy, and Sadler knew that Aunt Betsy had betrayed her.

Rather than think any more about Keynes, he decided

to piece together what he could remember about Betsy. Keynes had sent him off to the village Post Office with a parcel for London and he walked slowly, so preoccupied with his thoughts that he went past the Post Office and almost through the village before he remembered the package and turned round.

There had been the shop first of all. A big shop with a shiny wooden floor, smelling of camphor. And rows and rows of little drawers, some just above the floor, accessible to his inquisitive hands and holding, he knew, untold treasures. Very occasionally, he'd managed to pull one of the drawers out and spill its contents on to the floor – buttons or ribbons or cards of poppers and hooks and eyes, bundles of elastic, balls of darning wool. But then he'd be snatched away, held firmly on his mother's knee, fidgeting there, growing hot and wet and thirsty. The talk had gone on and on, interrupted now and then when a customer came in, and out would come the bales of material, fingered and taken to the daylight, finally unrolled in great coloured rivers on the long counter. The shop had been a tantalizing prison, a treasure chest of untouchable things, including, alas, the salmon-pink lady in a bride's gown who stood in the window.

And Betsy. What sign had there been that her mouth that was never still, the red mouth that spilled out a waterfall of words, would one day utter a betrayal? Had it indeed ever been uttered? Or was it something more hidden than words and more terrible? When Jack thought of her face – and he remembered it quite clearly – he saw it smiling. It smiled and smiled on them, on him and Annie and her quiet utterances and then it was gone. He knew it had existed. If the shop hadn't been real (and because, after a while, they never went there again, he began to wonder about this), the teashop was.

It had been an ordinary day off, starting early as usual because all the servants, except Mr Knightley, worked till breakfast time on their days off, and following the pattern that such days took – Jack being dressed up in his best and walking hand in hand with Annie down the long drive to catch the nine o'clock bus into town. On the way, Annie promised him treacle tart for lunch. She said they'd spend the morning looking at the shops as it was near Christmas and then they'd meet Aunt Betsy at twelve, in the teashop.

They arrived first, on the dot of twelve, and waited. Jack was hungry and a lady in black kept on coming up and asking them what they wanted and each time she came Annie said: 'I think we'll wait a bit longer.'

'Ma . . .'

'We're waiting for Aunt Betsy, Jack.'

'Couldn't I . . .'

'She'd think we were horrible if we ate before she came.'

So by the time she arrived with her smile, he hated her. She smelled of perfume, obliterating as she breezed in the smells of the teashop.

'Hello little Jacko!'

But the lady in black saved him by coming up again, not polite any more, quite rude this time, thrusting a menu card into Betsy's hand before she'd arranged herself on her chair, then standing by the table, refusing to go before they'd told her what they wanted to eat. Annie ordered Welsh rarebit for him and treacle tart to follow.

'No tart today.'

'Jackie, no treacle tart.'

So now the day was spoiled. He'd quite liked the lady in black to start with, but suddenly he hated her. As if sounding out his doom, he heard Annie say: 'He'll have rhubarb and custard.'

But the Welsh rarebit came quite quickly and it was nice. He felt his anger begin to slide away as he ate it. By the time he'd finished he felt quite happy again and wanted to talk. But as usual, even as she ate, Betsy's mouth was pouring out a torrent of chatter, pausing only for a smile and a nod or a 'did you, Bets?' from Annie to go rushing on, an impenetrable flood. It seemed to Jack that everyone else in the teashop was caught and swirled along in it, their own safe harbours of conversation abandoned. And then, quite suddenly, it stopped and, from watching the other people, Jack turned back to see Betsy with her face bright red, looking away from his mother whose eyes were wide, wide and her mouth gaping. There was absolute silence. Knives and forks clinking, but no other sound. He panicked. Before he had noticed it, he was up and tugging at Annie's arm.

'Let's go, Ma.'

But instead of getting up she just patted his hand.

'It's all right, love.'

He stood by her, not knowing what to do. Slowly, the sound of conversation started up again and then, with his head turned away, he heard Betsy say: 'It was none of my doing, Annie. I told John, I've a right to choose whom I please. But he says no. And honest, Annie, I don't know why, but I couldn't keep on at him, because what if he turned round and said no wedding then?'

'But we've been friends a long time, Betsy.'

'I know. That's what I told him. I told him it didn't matter to me what you'd done, we were still friends.'

'So?'

'So he said . . . what I told you . . . he said he didn't want me associating with you any more, that's what he said.'

'He's got pretensions, has your John Thomas.'

'No. It's just that he doesn't know you, that's all. It makes all the difference to things when you know someone.'

The rhubarb and custard came. The lady in black put it down in front of Jack with a smile. And that was all he remembered. He couldn't remember saying goodbye to

Betsy and in the afternoon, quite a fine one, they went down to the canal to look at the houseboats and he forgot about her. An old man popped up from one of the boats and invited Jack to come and have a look at it and Annie sat on the bank waiting for him till the old man tired of his questions and told him to run along.

After that day, Betsy with her red mouth and all her thousands of words disappeared. They quite often went to the teashop again, but she never came. Jack hadn't liked her, but friends were important, he sensed, like collections of fag cards, and as far as he could tell, Betsy was the only one his mother had ever had.

Jack posted the parcel for London, enjoying, as he entered the Post Office, its musty smell. Mrs Hood, sparrow-like behind her grid, always took off her glasses when someone came in, to make sure she knew whether to smile or not before she put them on again to read the labels on the old books she kept her stamps in. She reserved one of her nicest smiles for 'the little ones', as she called children, kept pieces of liquorice (that often went stale when days went past and no 'little ones' came in) in a bag under the counter to push under the grid to them with the change. She disapproved of children running errands, told her sister Mabel she considered it only fair to pay them as one would a servant – hence the sweets. She smelt of lavender and there was a compact greyness about her that Jack liked. His only regret was that it was liquorice, not barley sugar that came nudging towards him.

'Why don't you keep barley sugar, Mrs Hood?'

'What, dear?'

'It'd be nice if you had barley sugar.'

'Would it?'

'I think you should.'

'Well, it's always been liquorice. The little ones seem to like it.'

'I like barley sugar better.'

'Well, I could buy both, I suppose, couldn't I?'

'It might be too expensive, wouldn't it?'

Mrs Hood smiled. 'I'll see what I can do.'

It was always blinding, the sunshine, when you came out into it again after the darkness in the Post Office and Jack had begun to wonder how Mrs Hood's eyes, pale as they were, could adjust themselves to its brilliance. He worried that all the years of taking them backwards and forwards from dark to light, not to mention the on-off, on-off of the spectacles, were slowly dimming their sight.

This thought saddened him as he retraced his steps up the village street, and to brush it aside he let himself turn his attention to Keynes.

It was nice the way Keynes had encouraged him. None of the masters at school had ever said they'd like to see him get on. He'd stayed near the bottom of the class and no one seemed to notice, let alone tell him he might do well if he tried. And now, after those years of being the 'stick man' and the 'shiny man', someone was saying to him 'be good, Jack Sadler, and I'll give you a leg up, set you above the pigeons, above Cook with her piled hair, to where you and I can pretend to talk as equals.' The only trouble was, he couldn't bring himself to like Keynes. The man had a red face and neck and very red hands for which Jack pitied him. But the thought that any part of them might one day touch him made him shudder. No, if success lay in the caresses of Keynes's hands, Jack was wistfully aware that he could never let it come.

'Mr Sadler!'

Mrs Moore had come running. Sadler blinked, as if on waking, saw the orchard spread out all around him.

'What is it, Mrs Moore?'

'Reverend Chapman on the telephone.'

Sadler chuckled.

'Trust you to run – for the vicar!'

'He'd like a word, Sir.'

'Tell him it'd spoil my walk, will you?'

'Mr Sadler . . .'

'I'd never get out again, would I, if I had to go in for the telephone?'

'Sir . . .'

'Ask him what he wants and tell him to be so godly as to ring later.'

'Very good.'

She turned with a sniff. A sniff a bit like Vera's, expressing supreme disgust. What unkindnesses, he wondered, are dealt to aging women, the thin ones particularly it seemed, that make them turn to Jesus. Running downhill from fifty and all they can see is the church spire. Doesn't happen to a man – or at least to none Sadler had ever met – and certainly not to himself. So odd, they were, women. So terribly, pathetically afraid. All of different things, of course, but each one rapt in pursuit of safe havens. And the Church was the most obvious, the most accessible and the only one run exclusively by men. So there so many of them ran, believing perhaps in the infinite divisibility of the rock of Peter, hopeful that in men like the Reverend Chapman a splinter of it lay.

Not Madge, though.

'Geoffrey will insist,' she told Sadler one afternoon, 'on my going to church. Just to keep up appearances. And it does seem so very unnecessary, hypocritical even, don't you think, Sadler?'

'Well, I'll confess I never got on with Jesus myself.'

'Didn't you? Oh that *is* comforting!'

And they'd had a laugh the two of them, conspirators, 'sharing a joke'. And a glass of sherry. The Colonel was away on one of his visits to London and at five o'clock in the afternoon Madge had poured Sadler some of her best sherry from the decanter he always polished so nicely, and asked him to sit down.

'Tell me, Sadler, what do you believe in?'

No one else that he'd ever met would have asked him such a question, or if they had, would never have looked, as she did, for a serious, considered answer.

'Truth,' Sadler said.

'Oh that's lovely and vague! We're all in search of different truths, aren't we? Truth about the universe, truth about Right and Wrong, truth about ourselves. "Know thyself" someone said, didn't they? Who was that?'

'I don't know, Madam.'

'Well, it was a very important thing to say, I think. Everyone should start by trying to find out the truth about themselves. But what I want to know, although I realize it's very impertinent of me, is what *matters* to you?'

Sadler was conscious that he was leaning very heavily on his stick. The end had dug itself right into the turf. He tugged it out and walked on through the orchard, then down, as he had planned, towards the stream.

The last time he'd been there was the morning the estate agent had come, some weeks ago now. He'd come unasked-for and unannounced, driving a red sports car.

'All right with you, Sir, if I have a quick look round?'

'What d'you want to do that for?'

'Interest mainly, Sir. We like to keep tabs on everything in the neighbourhood. And I'd heard a rumour you were thinking . . .'

'It's not for sale.'

'No, no. Fine.'

'Nothing much to see – just empty rooms.'

'Fine.'

'You're fond of cars, are you?'

'I beg your pardon, Sir?'

'It's a very smart colour, I suppose, red.'

'Oh Matilda. Well, she goes, you know . . .'

Sadler had chuckled, pleased with the little blush he'd sent creeping up the young man's neck, enjoying himself more than he had for some time. And then the agent had pulled out a pocket tape recorder and begun talking softly to it: 'Large entrance hall, parquet flooring, leading east to drawing room, large, 25 feet plus into bay . . .' And Sadler's chuckle had turned into a laugh that had made him cough.

He'd tried to hide until the agent had gone. He'd taken the dog and wandered out to where he stood now. But half an hour later, just as he was beginning to get cold, the young man had come striding towards him.

'Hallo again, Sir.'

Sadler nodded.

'Mind if I have a word before I go?'

'Help yourself.'

'It's a very fine property. Been in the family long?'

'Not my family. I used to work here, that's all.'

The young man coughed. 'But you are the owner?'

'Yes, it's mine now.'

'And you're not sure you want to sell?'

'I know I don't want to sell!'

'No, I see. Well, that's a shame really. Of course I'd have to do a thorough survey before I could give you an accurate figure, but I'd say you'd get fifty or sixty for it.'

Sadler laughed. 'There's probably less days left in me than that!'

'Oh come on, Sir.'

'I'm not that stupid, either. What good's money in the bank if you've got no home?'

'You could buy a smaller place.'

'For dying in?'

He coughed again. 'No, well fine. Well, I'm sorry to have taken up your time. Perhaps you'll think about it, though. I know a couple of people who might be interested.'

And suddenly Sadler was angry. So cocksure, the agent was. His car and him – both anti-social pieces of machinery and Sadler wanted them gone.

'Listen to me,' he blurted out, 'you won't get me out, Sonny! I'm rooted – see!' He drove his stick into the ground. 'And I'm not budging. So drive your nice car up to London and go and pester the life out of some old thing in Barnes or Islington or wherever it is you people make your profits, but you leave me alone!'

He'd felt ashamed, but only a little, as the young man strode obediently away. Then he sat down. The pain of his anger had made him feel sick.

Sadler shivered. You couldn't stand still for long, in spite of the sun, without feeling cold. Wander on then, going nowhere as usual, unless perhaps to see the show the crocuses were putting on. He looked round for the dog but couldn't see him. Always a difficult moment, that, because the dog had no name he could call. Sadler spat, moistened his lips ready for a whistle, when he saw the dog no more than a few yards from him, watching him.

'Come on,' he said. And the dog got up, a bit shakily, wagging the tuft and steering himself carefully through the long grass. 'We'll go and look at the flowers.'

Years ago, the gardeners had planted crocuses the whole length of the drive. Wren used to say they were his two favourite colours – purple and yellow. And people even wandered up from the village to steal a look at their brief flowering. Now there were only a few clumps, a patch here and there often hidden by the new year's growth of weeds.

'Aren't they a picture?' said a voice in Sadler's ear. It was Mrs Moore with her coat on, ready to scuttle off home. Sadler was disappointed.

'You didn't stay long today, Mrs Moore.'

'It's gone ten, Mr Sadler. And I promised my sister . . .'

'Oh well. I'll see you tomorrow.'

'Not tomorrow, Sir. Tomorrow's Sunday.'

'Is it? I lose track these days.'

'Yes. The Day of Rest, and I can't say I'm not thankful for it.'

Sadler nodded.

'Oh and I meant to tell you, Sir, the Reverend Chapman would like to call on you about tea-time, if that would be convenient.'

'I don't suppose I'll be going anywhere.'

And then she was off. Little hasty steps, one two, one two, one two in her neat brown shoes. One two, one two, one two, one two, gone.

Imagine, Sadler thought, loving her. He pitied the man who could shoulder that burden, who'd have his soul pecked at day after day, wake with her creased elbow in his shoulder, spend his love in a body that had resisted and resisted and turned away thankfully to God. Better to be alone, really, than watched by that accusing eye. And yet what if she never came back, if no one came? What if they just left him there with the dust and dirt and his memories?

He felt very tired. 'We've done enough walking,' he said to the dog, 'let's go back.' And he was glad when he stepped into the warm kitchen, all its surfaces tidy and scrubbed now, even the teapot washed up and put away. He took off his boots and hung his coat up, but forgot the woolly scarf dangling round his neck. The dog went straight to its place by the Aga and lay down thankfully. Too old it was really to go for walks, its little legs too stiff at the joints.

'I know,' said Sadler, 'I know. But don't you dare die.'

He sat down at the kitchen table, in a familiar attitude, resting his arms on it. There was an old wireless, hideous sack of a thing squatting on top of the fridge, but still obediently sending out crackly versions of the BBC's tidings, and Sadler thought he might switch it on. There weren't many of the songs they sang these days that he liked, but now and then one stuck in his head and humming it would cheer him up. But he only remembered them if they amused him and the last one had been more than two years ago:

> Going up to the Spirit in the Sky,
> That's where I go when I die,
> When I die and they lay me to rest
> Gonna go to the place that's the best!

He'd made Mrs Moore listen to the words of this song one morning, he chuckling, she sour, glowering into her tea.

'It's a good song, isn't it, Mrs Moore?'

'I've never cared for pops and that.'

'Don't you like the words, though?'

'Well, they're all speaking American, aren't they? You can't understand them half the time.'

'I quite like that song.'

'Too jerky for me.'

Mrs Moore had never been more certain about anything than that the singer of the song would never get to heaven, and Sadler had thought, Lord, what an arrogance there seems to be in people who think God loves them. Like members of a club. Certain habits, they said, excluded you. Forgetting, though, that Jesus kept company with publicans and sinners, and nowadays, Sadler had laughingly suggested, it'd be republicans and singers, wouldn't it? But not a ghost of a smile in her cheek, merely reproach in her eyes for his feeble joke and a few words spat out with venom: 'You ought to go to *church*!'

He had, regularly, long ago. While in the service of Milord, the servants all went to church. Her ladyship expected it, would glance behind her, counting heads as the Reverend Stooks and his choir of four (five occasionally with the addition of Charlie Stooks, the vicar's youngest son, red in the face and smiling like a nervous bride) measured out the fifteen paces to the altar steps. Right at the back, Cook always wanted to clap but restrained herself by adjusting her hatpins instead.

That church, smelling of the dusty seeds that filled the hassocks, was always full on a Sunday morning, often so crammed with people that Jack was squeezed up tight against his mother. In the shelter of her arm, he'd looked up at the incredible blue just behind Christ's head on the window, found it like no other blue he'd ever seen. Where, he wanted to ask her – in what mysterious corner of his being – had the man who made the window discovered it? In Art at school he'd striven unsuccessfully to find that blue, week after week. Something more beautiful than the sky and yet containing the sky: his sky.

Jack had quite a good voice, so Mrs Dean said, and he'd been proud enough of it to sing out when the congregation shuffled to its feet for a hymn. And he secretly longed to come walking down the nave with the choir, envied the ludicrous Charlie Stooks his lace ruff. He didn't remember ever thinking about God. And if God had been there in those crowded pews, in those facets of blue, He had disappeared after that.

'No insistence is made here,' Keynes told Sadler, 'on the servants attending worship. Everyone does as they please, provided they're not required for domestic duty at that time on a Sunday. I myself am not a church-going man.'

So church was forgotten. 'I myself,' it seemed the pigeons had cooed one by one, 'am not a church-going, am not a church-going, am not a church-going girl.' Sadler wondered if they stayed away to please Keynes.

'Why don't you go to church, Mary?' he'd asked her one Sunday.

'Church?' she said, 'whatever next!'

So that was it, then. Here, you weren't expected to go

and stand under a blue window. God was gone. You still said a prayer each night that began 'God bless Ma', but you never thought about the God part of it any more.

Until one day in 1930 He summoned you again. He brought you back to His door after all that time. A spring day in April, a breeze like a child's breath. And there you stood, obedient as a child, and because someone had told you all that while ago that God is Love, ashamed, mortally ashamed of your anger. Summoned by letter. A shaky, almost indecipherable hand, Milady's, nearing her seventy-ninth year and widowed now, speaking of her sorrow, her real sorrow 'because I'd grown so fond of Annie your dear Mother, who has been such a loyal servant to me these past years', and it was God who passed back into your head, the friend you'd abandoned when you were young and who now exacted a price for your disloyalty.

There was laurel by the cemetery gate. You touched one of the leaves, rubbed it between finger and thumb as you waited for the people to arrive. You stood and waited and waited and no one came. Then you went inside and you looked up at the fretted blue behind Christ's head on the window and you wept. Ghastly, uncontrollable, convulsive sobs that made you retch, and you knelt down, not because you wanted to kneel to God, but because you couldn't stand up, because you had to hold on to something, hearing, feeling nothing but the grief that swelled and heaved inside you. Then there was a cold, soft touch on your shoulder, a touch you knew was meant to heal and comfort, but which only made you aware of your shame, silenced you, but left your body rocking back and forth, back and forth, unable to be still, but searching now somewhere for a name, the name of the hand that touched it, aware that there was a time when it would have recognized that hand, known that name. And little by little, you brought yourself back to stillness, the hand stayed on your shoulder and in your head you said to it, give me time, stay and comfort me till I can look up and see your face, because I know that when I look up I'll know your face, even though I haven't seen it for so long and then I'll remember . . . But you had remembered the name: Stooks. You'd conjured it from somewhere, found it through your feeble fumblings in absolute darkness and run to it as towards a tiny prick of light. Stooks. And with the name came the remembrance of a face. You saw it clearly now, just as it used to be, could even picture it standing above you and smiling. Your body was still now, still and silent and light was seeping back under your eyelids. You reached out a hand and held on to the hard wood of the back of the pew and you turned your face as you felt the hand lift off your back and looked up. And you saw a stranger.

Sadler was staring at the wire meshing on the front of the old wireless. His eyes had fixed themselves on to this square, following intently the journeying of the brown threads that had woven it. His eyes were dry and smarting so he closed them. He began wondering why he'd been looking at the wireless, and then he remembered that he'd been going to turn it on. Good idea to turn it on, he thought now. Far better to listen to a song than to all the snatches of sound he'd been drubbing up in his head.

V

'Cor!' Tom said.

Wren had been into town, driving Madge who wanted to do some shopping and he'd returned with Tom's *Champion*, as promised.

'Thanks Mr Wren.'

'Last one in the shop.'

'Cor. Was it?'

'Lucky to get it. I reckon that might have gone if I'd been a bit later.'

'I'm glad you got it.'

'Good, is it?'

'Yeah.'

'Can't remember what I read when I was a lad.'

'Comics, didn't you?'

'I can't remember anything like that.'

'What then?'

'Books, I suppose, just books.'

'My Ma says no one's got time for books, 'cos of the war.'

'That's probably true, Tom. There must be a lot of things people don't have time for now.'

'Why aren't you in the war, Mr Wren?'

'Too old, son, too old to fight.'

Here was a straight answer, one Tom understood. Rare, though, in the life he now led, which seemed to be full of confusions, of questions that went unanswered. At home, there'd been his Ma to ask about things and he'd always believed in the truth of her answers, never once

111

questioned it. And when there wasn't his Ma, there was Martha-Ann, who always started her answers with a reassuring, 'Well, Tommy, you know what I'd say to that?' And when there wasn't Martha-Ann, there was an 'auntie' of some shape or colour. All of which had led Tom to believe that only women knew the truth about things, that in them resided most of the world's wisdom. But Vera had disappointed him. So busy, she always seemed to be – her thin arms sinewy from the unceasing activity, backwards and forwards with the rolling pin, round and round with the spoon – that questions seemed to get in her way and she'd trip over them. Like on the afternoon, during Tom's first week, when, sitting in the kitchen watching her, he'd felt homesick and said:

''Ow long am I staying 'ere, Vera?'

'What, love?'

She was dusting a pie with sugar. She'd made a flower out of the bits of pastry left over and stuck it on the top.

'How long am I staying 'ere?'

'Rest of your life, I wouldn't wonder.'

'Why?'

'What, duck?'

She wasn't listening. She was carrying her pie to the oven.

'Why?'

She was holding the pie in one hand, opening the oven door with the other. But then, just as she was about to answer him, she bumped her pie with the oven door and the flower fell off on to the floor.

'Flamin' 'ell!'

'*Why*, Vera?'

'Cos Mr 'itler sez you must.'

''E never . . . '

'Ask no questions and get told no flippin' lies, duck.'

And that was really disappointing. Schoolmasters, he'd noticed, often slithered round questions by asking you one

112

back, but women usually told you something you could believe in.

Tom opened his *Champion* as soon as Wren had gone. He'd been sitting on his bed most of the afternoon, waiting for it. The last one he'd seen had been three weeks ago and it was in that issue they'd announced a new adventure series with a new hero, Rockfist Rogan of the RAF. He'd missed two weeks. Two Fridays had come and gone and he and Rockfist were still unacquainted. But now, on page five, there he was!

Biff! Thud! Biff!

'Gosh Rockfist, I don't know how you've got the energy to hit that punch bag around!'

Flight Lieutenant Rogan of the Royal Air Force, known to his pals as Rockfist because of his boxing prowess, grinned at Curly Hooper and continued his vigorous punching.

He ducked, weaved, dodged on his toes, hurling punches at the spinning bag as if he meant to batter it to bits.

Thud! Biff! Thud!

Rockfist's blows set the bag swinging wildly.

At that moment, the door opened and a staff officer stepped in, walking unsuspectingly into the path of the flying bag.

The full weight of the bag took him in the chest.

'Oof!'

'Wow!'

The newcomer was flung back against the wall. Rockfist stood rooted to the spot in dismay.

'Oh gosh —' he began.

The bag was swinging back. Rockfist was too surprised to notice it. It swept up and clonked him on the chin.

'Ugh!' he cried, and hit the floor with a thump.

Tom laughed. And an hour later he had read it all. Not just the story about Rockfist Rogan. He'd been on tour with the Roving Rovers, Fireworks Flynn the Wizard Sports Master had captured a mystery sharpshooter,

Colwyn Dane, Mark Grimshaw's famous 'tec, had solved the Riddle of the Vanished Speedster and the Mantamer from Muskrat had won again. Everything was right in the world of *Champion*. So Tom had gone to sleep on his bed and the *Champion* had fallen on to the floor. His tea-time had come and gone and Vera, having one of her bad days, had sent Sadler off in search of him.

'Tea's all ready, Mr Sadler, but I won't 'ave it sitting on the table till dinner-time. He can go without.'

Sadler went up to the coconut matting landing. Tom's room was two doors along from his own, smaller than his, but with the same view over the orchard from its high window. There were no pictures in it, only a little embroidered motto: *Friday's child is full of grace*.

'I wasn't born on a Friday,' Tom had remarked.

'What day were you born on, Tom?'

'Dunno. Not a Friday.'

Sadler knocked before going into Tom's room. The boy was entitled to the illusion that this at least belonged to him and that he had some rights over it. But there was no sound at all from inside it, so Sadler opened the door quietly and went in. Tom was lying on his back with his fist above his head.

'Tom,' Sadler whispered. But he didn't stir.

Sadler looked at him and thought, I could reach out and touch him and he wouldn't know. Then he saw Tom's *Champion* lying on the floor and bent down and picked it up. The word CATAPULTS in large letters in an advertisement box caught his attention. A special offer, it said, for four and ninepence, carriage paid. 'Polished aluminium fork with wide spread, square quarter-inch elastic. Leather sling. State age when ordering.' Sadler had always been able to file things in his memory, hadn't needed to write everything down like the Colonel. So he noted the address and the sum of four and ninepence.

Tom woke up to see Sadler standing by his bed, looking

at his comic.

'That's mine,' he said.

Sadler smiled.

It was some weeks before the catapult Sadler had ordered arrived, and it was during this time that Tom discovered the ballroom.

The ballroom was a huge, rectangular room, originally painted light green, but with brownish patches now, where the damp had seeped into the walls.

'I don't know,' said Madge, 'how long it is since anyone gave a ball in there. The Colonel and I gave one in about about 1930, but it was perfectly ghastly! Muriel Portsmouth drank too much and vomited on the bandstand and someone started a conga round the garden – a conga! – the most ridiculous thing I've ever seen, and all my roses were ruined. I think I must have put my foot down after that.'

It had become a place to put things in. Things you didn't want any more. It was chilly and dark because all the windows were shuttered.

Tom had managed to open the shutters on four of the windows and there, with an old sofa, broken lamps, a picnic hamper, photo albums, a garden bed on wheels, empty picture frames and piles of magazines and newspapers he decided to pitch his camp. The room became his den. He wanted to have his meals in there, but Vera said: 'Good 'eavens, duck, you don't imagine me an' Betty's going ter traipse up there with your dinner, do you?'

He would have slept in there, only Sadler said it was too cold. But it was his place, and he shared it with five 'others'.

He discovered the 'others' the day he discovered the ballroom. Five flat men, made of thin wood, painted but faded now with age and sunshine, their eyes pale as mothballs and their bodies shot through with tiny holes.

The Colonel had set up a rifle range years ago in the

field above the orchard. There had been one or two of his army cronies who'd been keen and he'd had the figures built so that they could hold competitions. They only held one competition and the Colonel won, so he thought he'd stop it at that, quit while he was ahead. But the flat men had stood out in the range for years, growing paler and paler as seasons passed and no one shot at them, until one summer Madge had hit upon the idea of lending them to the local fête. They were loaded on to a lorry and driven off to the football ground where the Hentswell fête was held. They were shot at for a whole afternoon, a hot Sunday in August, and then that same lorry brought them back, and Sadler and the lorry driver carried them one by one into the ballroom. Here Tom found them and stood them up round the room and gave them names – Ginger, Soapy, Norman (his favourite), Hans (a German) and Roger. They all looked exactly the same. The only way to tell them apart was by the different patterning of little holes in them. But Tom told Sadler countless things about them as individuals, a layer of complex detail covering their sameness, obliterating it.

'Roger's an orphan,' he said, 'that's why he had spots.' Roger's face, it was true, was horribly pitted with holes.

'Norman's my best one.'

'Why, Tom?'

'Well, he listens to me.'

'What about Hans?'

'He's a German.'

'What's he doing in England?'

'He's a prisoner.'

'Oh.'

'And the others don't like him because 'e's a German and that.'

'And Ginger?'

'He's called after Ma's cat. Cats are his favourite animal. He has cat exhibitions, see?'

Tom had picked some of the largest leaves he could find off the virginia creeper that grew outside the ballroom, and laid them out, evenly spaced, on the long table. They were different shades of red and orange.

'That's Ginger's cat exhibition. You can judge it if you like.'

So Sadler judged it, selecting three leaves and designating them first, second and third.

'What can we give as prizes?'

'Pick something out of Soapy's shop.'

Soapy had been stood in a corner and at his feet had been laid all the smaller items Tom had found – broken crockery, dusty old decanters, an alarm clock, a cutlery tray, two piles of the *Illustrated London News*, an empty jewel case, an assortment of lamps.

'He sells those things.'

Sadler fumbled in his pocket for money.

'You don't have to buy them, Jack.'

Sadler caught his breath. It was years now since anyone had called him by his name. He wanted to thank Tom. He wanted to hold the boy to him and tell him that although he wouldn't understand, it meant a lot to him. He found sixpence and held it out.

'You don't have to,' said Tom, 'it's only a game.'

It wasn't that Ginger and company were substitutes for real friends Tom had known and was missing. He hadn't made any real friends. He'd played with the other boys in his street and in the playground at school, but the boundaries of their friendship were drawn by the lines of chalk which mapped out their games. When the game ended, when the whistle blew or someone's Ma called out, they shrugged him off. There never seemed to be any use for him outside the game.

He had gone with a crowd of boys from school one Saturday to a fair. But instead of riding on the roundabouts, all the others had wanted to do was to watch the

117

girls' skirts blowing up as they went round. Tom had got bored with staring at girls' thighs, wandered off and found a stall where you could win a goldfish by bouncing a ping-pong ball into a glass jar. He had thirteen goes, spent all the money his Ma had given him, and still the ping-pong ball wouldn't stay in the jar. With his money gone, he could only stare miserably at the amazing fish. He could just imagine how it would feel to carry one home.

'Go on then, mate,' the stall owner said.

Tom looked up, unbelieving. Then he saw the man pick up one of the bowls with a goldfish in it and hand it to him.

'Cor!' said Tom. 'Thanks, mister.'

He carried it home, the other boys forgotten. He carried it so carefully that not a drop of water was spilt. He waited up, staring at it for hours until his Ma got in and he could show it to her.

'Go *on*!' she said, 'you must've got one in. You never get something for nothing.'

It wasn't nothing, he explained, it was all the money he had. He probably could have bought a goldfish three times over with that money. But she still didn't believe him, until the following morning when they woke to find the goldfish floating, belly up, dead as you like.

'Oh well,' she said, 'that explains it, don't it? 'E must have know the poor little sod was on its last legs.'

No. Friends had been no good to Tom. Ginger and Soapy and Norman and Hans and the orphaned Roger were better than friends. They were better than animals or fish. They could be soldiers if you chose, they could be kings. And more than anything, you were indispensable to them. You held their existence in your head.

The days weren't long any more. The days flew.

'I dunno,' said Vera one morning to Sadler, 'he's made strides, that boy.'

He didn't hang around the kitchen any more, asking questions and getting in her way.

'He's happy now,' Sadler told her.

The weather was getting very cold. It rained a lot in November, and Madge and the Colonel spent more and more of each day together, because, they seemed to be saying, what with the confusing news from France and the rain falling, they needed to comfort each other. They'd sit and talk or do crosswords or play Gin Rummy. And when the news came on the wireless, Madge would sometimes reach out and hold the Colonel's hand. She was waiting, she said, for something to happen. She'd begun to feel uneasy, as if they were falling silently, those German bombs, from an unimaginable height, taking days and days to come whispering down.

'Come on, old thing,' the Colonel would say, 'you're losing your sense of reality.'

And Madge thought, yes, that's just it. Because it *is* unreal, sitting behind our blacked out windows, with the BBC telling us one thing one day and another the next. 'It's not like in 1914,' she said, 'with all those bands.'

They didn't often see Tom. They heard him (such an unfamiliar sound, his high voice, in that house), and one morning, feeling she ought to do something for him, Madge came into the kitchen when he was having his breakfast and said: 'I'm going into town today, Tom, in the car. If you'd like to come with me, we'll see what we can find to buy you.'

'All right,' said Tom.

'You go and get ready when you've finished your breakfast and be thinking what you might like. We'll be leaving at half past nine.'

Tom sat in front with Wren, Madge behind. Wren guided the little car even more slowly and carefully than usual because of the rain and it took them nearly an hour to get there, an hour spent in almost total silence. Only Wren ventured along a couple of conversational paths:

'Terrible weather for flying,' he remarked, but his voice

was drowned by the whine of the windscreen wipers so Madge didn't hear and Tom was preoccupied scanning the hedgerows for German helmets. Later, when they were entering Norwich, Wren said to Tom: 'I'd go to Denny's if I were you.'

'What's Denny's?'

'It's a sort of bicycle shop, I think you'd call it, but they got a nice collection of odds and ends in there, torches and pocket knives and . . .'

'Torches are no good. You can't get no more number eight batteries, that's what my Ma said.'

'I think Denny's is a good idea, though,' said Madge. 'Let's drop you off there while I go and do my shopping and by the time I get back you'll have chosen something, won't you?'

'I could look in some other shops, couldn't I?'

'Well, of course, go wherever you like, but we'll meet back at Denny's.'

Denny's was, as Wren had said, a bicycle shop, and the first thing that caught Tom's eye was a bicycle.

'Thinking about Christmas then, are you son?'

Mr Denny had been watching Tom fingering the bike. Now he moved out from behind his counter, smiling.

'How much is it?' Tom asked.

'Seven pounds thirteen, that one.'

Tom walked away from it and began looking up and down the shelves. Mr Denny moved up behind him. Because you never knew with young lads in a shop like his. My kind of stock's so vulnerable, he always explained, it's tempting providence you might say, but what can I do? You've got to display these kind of items. Mind you, they seldom take things when they come in on their own. It's the gangs you have to watch – dare each other, I suppose.

'Looking for anything special, son?'

'They said I could choose something.'

'Did they now? Well, and how much did they say you

120

could spend?'

'Dunno, Sir.' (Told that he should address the Colonel as 'Sir', Tom now used it on everyone.)

'A birthday, is it?'

'No. They just said I could have something.'

Mr Denny sniffed. The boy's voice, the length of his sleeves, too short by several inches, his reference to 'they' – all spelled 'vacuee' in his opinion. And his opinion of 'vacuees' was low, decidely low, 'because I've seen with my own eyes the trouble they can cause and the dirt on them . . .' He'd need watching, this one, and closely, Mr Denny decided. Best to get him out of the shop as quickly as he could.

'I can tell you what I've been selling a lot of,' he said, 'catapults.'

He produced a box of them.

'Superior type, aluminium, these. Very popular with the older age bracket.'

'I had one of them once, but it got broke,' said Tom.

He didn't like Mr Denny. It would have been nice to look up and down the shelves, but not when he was being followed like this and shown things he didn't want. A man came into the shop, asking for a valve for a bicycle pump, so while Mr Denny was putting on his glasses to look for the appropriate box, he scuttled out into the rain. Mr Denny took off his glasses and smiled at the customer.

'You can tell 'em a mile off, can't you? Funny, isn't it?'

But Tom did ride home clutching a parcel. When Madge had come back, her red umbrella buffetted by the driving rain, her stockings spattered, she'd been surprised to see Tom standing outside Denny's shop, sheltered a bit against the wall, but his hair and clothes very wet.

'You should have waited inside,' Madge said. 'I'm sure Mr Denny wouldn't have minded.'

'Couldn't we go to some other shop?'

'Yes, of course we can, if you like. Didn't you see

anything in Denny's?'

'I know what I'd like,' Tom said flatly. 'I'd like a drawing book and some colours.'

Once back at the house, he ran inside before anyone could tell him to be sure and take off his wet things. He went straight to the ballroom, running all the way, eager to sit down at the long table and begin.

Tom always drew what he could see. When he tried to sketch out something that was just in his head it seemed to go wrong. At school they'd all been asked one morning to paint pictures of their mothers, and Tom had gone to work confidently, certain that what he could 'see' in his mind his hand could reproduce. But the painting, it seemed to him, turned out nothing like his Ma. She stared out at him with a blank look, and her mouth – something had gone very wrong with her mouth – it looked more like a wound.

So now he looked round the room and decided to start a picture of Hans, on whose head he'd put a china pot to act as a helmet. He drew him striding out, not standing, legs together, as he was, and he drew Roger and Norman a little way behind him whispering together. There was only one bit of pure invention in the picture: he drew in a small black dog and labelled him DICK. After that Dick became part of Tom's world. Sadler bought a cheap bowl for the dog and Tom painted his name on it.

Betty came and told him that his lunch was ready, but he asked her to tell Vera that he wasn't hungry.

'Suit yourself, Tom,' Betty chimed, 'but she'll be after you!'

He didn't mind. At home he'd always had to make do with five colours, rather short ones in a cheap box. Now he had a big, flat tin of sharp crayons, arranged so that dark blue faded into sky blue and sky blue into apple green and green into yellow and so on, right across to purple. Tom couldn't remember owning anything – except maybe the goldfish – he'd liked more. Even the paper Madge had bought him was of wonderful quality, thick and very white. He wanted to make picture after picture, so he sat there all afternoon and his wet coat and socks and shoes dried on him.

That day was Sadler's day off. He stayed in his room for most of the morning, glad he'd made no plans, feeling tired. Under his window, the fruit trees glistened in the rain, their leaves almost gone. Sadler wished he had a fire in his room, a warm centre to huddle by. The house was always deathly quiet up on his landing. Looking out was like being suspended in silence. And by noon, he found himself listening avidly for the sound of a voice, Tom's hopefully. But it was as if the whole house slept.

So Sadler did what he'd never intended to do: he went to the drawer where he kept his personal correspondence and picked up a letter that lay on top of the pile. Then he took down his mackintosh and went out.

He caught the twelve thirty bus into the village. Sitting at the back where it was the least draughty, he pulled the letter out of his pocket to read.

Dear Mr Sadler,

I haven't been up to the Hall again. I don't think Colonel and Mrs Bassett like me coming. I expect they find me terribly interfering. I don't mean to be, of course, I'm just doing a job. But I am anxious to know if everything is all right, because I feel very responsible for Tom, having persuaded the Bassetts to take him. This is why I am writing to you, and I hope you won't mind. Do you think you could find the time to visit me on one of your free days? There is a lot I would like to ask you and as I say I don't want to come up to the house too often.

I look forward to hearing from you,

    Yours sincerely

      Mary Reader   10 Wirrals Cottages,

                                            Hentswell

Sadler hadn't replied. He hadn't thought about the letter again until that morning had found him cold and a bit lonely and with nothing to do. He'd imagined suddenly that Miss Reader's cottage would be warm at least and that he could sit in front of a fire while he talked to her. And it was something to do. He never interfered with the rest of the staff on his days off. Let them muddle on without me, was his policy and he never strayed from it, even if he stayed in. On a fine day, he might have waited till Tom came back and gone for one of his walks with him, but the rain looked set in.

The bus got him to the village too quickly. When he got off, he stood for a while in the bus shelter, wondering if, after all, he'd just have a beer at The Fox and wait for the bus back. It was only the thought that he could warm himself by a fire that made him set off down the street.

Opening the door to him, seeing him standing hunched in his mac, Miss Reader found herself trembling. It was so unfair of him to surprise her like that. She hated surprises. She tried to steady herself as she took his mac and showed him into her living room. A bright fire burned there.

Sadler noticed her nervousness and was embarrassed by it.

'I won't stay long,' he said.

He went to the fire and stood in front of it, warming his hands.

'What can I get you?' Miss Reader asked. 'I always wish I was one of those people who made marvellous home-brewed wine, but I never seem to have time, and this kitchen is so tiny! But I've got sherry. You could have sherry if you like.'

Sadler accepted. He liked sherry. There was always a bottle for him and Vera at Christmas and the two of them drank it with relish, wondering why, when it was so enjoyable, they didn't do it more often.

Mary Reader had planned Sadler's visit. She'd

imagined how she would make him feel at home, make him see that she wanted to get to know him – as a friend, and some day, if he could come to believe in the friendship, as a lover. Tom was just an excuse, a very convenient one, for bringing him here. And now, there he stood, in her living room, but all she could find in her head were the wrong words.

'I'm afraid you quite surprised me! I was trying to do some baking, but I'm hopeless at it, I really am!'

'What were you making?'

'Oh it's called Madeira cake, I think. Mrs Dart next door gave me the recipe. But my cakes always turn out soggy, and it's not the oven or anything, it's me.'

She handed Sadler a glass of sherry.

'Aren't you going to have any?' he asked.

'Shall I? I can never make up my mind about it. Sometimes it seems to taste horrible.'

'Have half a glass with me, and then I'll be getting along.'

'Oh no. You mustn't go. You've hardly got here, and it isn't often I have a visitor. There were things I was going to ask you, I'm sure there were. I think I warned you in my letter, there were lots of things . . . and now I can't think of one.'

'About Tom?'

'Yes.'

'He's with me most of the time.'

'Yes, I thought that'd be it.'

'Doesn't fuss me. We're good friends.'

'I'm glad.'

'He's found quite a bit to interest him, too. The old ballroom up there's full of odds and ends they've put out of the way. Kids see a whole world in a place like that.'

'The Bassetts don't mind?'

'Oh no. They like to feel he's occupied.'

'Things are in such a muddle – with the schools. None

125

of them seems to know how many they can take. But we'll find a place for him after Christmas, I'll make myself responsible . . .'

'He'll survive.'

'If you could, of course, find the time to do a few lessons with him . . .'

'He's best doing what he wants.'

'Well, yes, I'm certain you're right. As long as he's not unhappy, that's our main concern, isn't it?'

Sadler said nothing and Miss Reader was anxious to scramble together some more words, but searched and found none. She hated the taste of her sherry, but sipped it for something to do, taking sip after sip until it was all gone.

'Well . . .' said Sadler.

'You must think me terrible,' she began in a rush, 'getting you here like this and not remembering any of the things I was going to say. I always find that if people take me by surprise I'm quite tongue-tied. My parents were always doing it, springing people on me, friends of theirs, people I couldn't get on with. It was terrible. Even when I wanted to like them, there was always someone to say something clever, just when I'd said something banal and everyone would laugh. I've always found it . . . so difficult . . . and I couldn't be more wrong for the job I do, when so much depends on being able to talk to people, to persuade them. I really couldn't be more wrong, don't you think?'

Sadler noticed that her hands were shaking and that her face worked itself into extraordinary contortions all the time.

She reminded him of a girl he'd met when he was working near Scarborough. Clare. She worked in a shop where he bought his tobacco. Clare Morley – or was it Mosley? Pretty till she spoke and then with the movements her face had to make to get the words out, suddenly ugly. She'd gone on and on at him, kept calling, kept sending him things, kept asking him why, when all the other men she'd liked had loved her, couldn't he love her? She wasn't a virgin, she whispered to him. Lost all that when she was still in school. And she wasn't one to start hearing wedding bells after the first kiss, like most of the girls she knew. So what was stopping him? What in the world could he be afraid of, when there she was fancying him like she'd never fancied anyone, mad for him and asking no promises from him, just his love. It was a persecution. Desire would never come, Sadler had known. Drunk or sober, he would never be able to make love to Clare. In the end, because he couldn't touch her, because he couldn't bear to touch any part of her, he had to tell her that he hated her, tell her and see her face crumple and watch the anger she felt rise until she struck out and hit him. He never saw her again. She disappeared. He asked no one where she had gone and no one told him. He was thankful.

Sadler brought his attention back to Miss Reader. She was looking at him quizzically, the flow of words stemmed, a kind of exhaustion in her eyes. He moved away from the fire. Really it had been his only reason for coming, but now he was finding it too hot.

'I've been thinking,' she began again, 'not so much about Tom as about you. I'd felt that . . . oh, I don't know what I felt, I just wanted to get to know you. And I don't usually. I can't bear it usually, the idea of getting to know someone. It always seems to take so long and leaves you feeling so puzzled.'

Sadler nodded. It was difficult to answer her. He didn't even know if she wanted an answer.

'But I thought it might have been nice, just to try, just to . . .'

He wanted to stop her talking now because he was embarrassed for her. How could she, with her seesaw of a voice, bear to humiliate herself?

'The war, you see. The war changes things, don't you think? It brings people together, breaks down barriers. It has to, doesn't it, because if we're all divided from each other even at home, how will we fight?'

Sadler just nodded.

'Well,' he said, 'no time to spend today. I'll have to be getting back.'

'Yes of course. I'm sorry. I didn't mean to pressure you. I hope you don't feel I was pressuring you, do you?'

He smiled at her.

'I enjoyed the sherry.'

It had almost stopped raining. A pale sun slanted down on to the street and it shone. Sadler felt his spirits soar as he stepped out into it and he walked, enjoying the fresh air, the few hundred yards to The Fox, where he ordered a beer.

He got back late, on impulse taking the bus to Norwich in the afternoon, spending the rest of the day looking round the market. Not so late that he couldn't serve dinner to the Colonel and Madge, though, because this was one of the Colonel's rules – everything had to be back to normal in the house by dinner time, or he couldn't eat.

There was a small package addressed to Sadler in the servants' hall and recognizing the name on the label, he knew it was the catapult he'd ordered for Tom. But the boy was in bed now. He'd give it to him in the morning.

As Sadler took the coffee into the drawing room, he noticed that a rough wind had begun to buffet the house. All you needed was a wind like that at this time of year to send the last leaves flying off. When it died down, winter would be there. Madge shivered by her fire.

'I forgot,' she said, 'to ask you, Sadler. Did you have a nice day?'

'Yes, thank you, Madam. I met our billeting officer in the village. She enquired after Tom.'

'What did you tell her?'

'I told her he was doing fine.'

'Good. He is, of course, isn't he, Sadler? I'm afraid he finds it very difficult to talk to me and the Colonel. I took him to Norwich today and he hardly said a word.'

'He talks to you, Sadler, doesn't he?' asked the Colonel.

'Yes Sir. When he feels like it.'

'Well, damn right! No sense in gabbling just for the sake of it. Worse than the silent ones, the gabblers.'

'He asked me for a drawing book,' said Madge.

'Did he, Madam? He told me once that he liked drawing.'

'Jolly good, I'd say,' beamed the Colonel. 'Budding artist in the family – make a nice change!'

Sadler was tired. He said goodnight, told Vera to go in a bit later for the coffee tray, and went upstairs. When he got to his landing, he noticed that there was a light under Tom's door. He considered going back down to get the catapult, but then he thought, no, better to wait till the morning when he can take it outside and play with it. But he knocked on Tom's door all the same. Sometimes Tom went to sleep with his light on, forgetting even to draw the blackout curtains.

'Who is it?' Tom called.

'It's me, Jack.'

When Sadler went in, he saw Tom lying on the floor in his vest and pants, propped up on one elbow which also held steady his drawing book. On the floor by him were his crayons and four pictures he'd already finished.

'I can draw Norman and them without looking now,' he announced.

'With your eyes shut?'

'Don't be soft! Without copying, I meant. Just from my head.'

'Let's see . . .'

'Look what she got me.'

129

He knelt up and held out the box of crayons for Sadler to see.

'That's nice.'

'Yeah.'

Sadler bent over him to look at his pictures. They were all of the 'others' – Hans in his helmet, Soapy with his shop, Ginger, Roger and Norman side by side.

'They're very good, Tom.'

'You don't think so, really.'

'I do. I think they're good pictures.'

Tom watched Sadler looking at his drawings.

'I hoped you'd come so as I could show you.'

'Did you? Well, I'm glad you've got a drawing book. I would have bought you one if you'd asked me.'

'*You* got no money, have you?'

'Enough to buy you that.'

Tom was sitting up now, watching the curtains move, listening to the wind.

'I don't like that,' he said after a while. 'It's spooky.'

'The wind?'

'I don't think it's just a wind. There's things out there, ain't there?'

'Only the usual things – trees and owls and —'

'I don't want to be in the dark.'

'There's nothing to hurt you, Tom. It's not even a storm.'

'I don't like it. I'm not going to sleep.'

'All right,' Sadler said, 'come on in to my room till it goes away.'

'Could I?'

Tom got into Sadler's bed and Sadler took his jacket and tie off and lay down beside him. They lay there in the darkness listening to the wind.

'I like it in your room,' Tom said.

'Do you? Well, I'll tell you,' Sadler whispered to him, 'when I was a kid. I used to share a bed no bigger than this with my Ma, whose name was Annie, in a room very like this one. There was even a picture in it a bit like the one on the wall just above us – two little kids on a seesaw in this green meadow – and my Ma used to say they'd put it there to remind me to work hard, like in the rhyme.'

'What rhyme?'

'Seesaw, Margery Daw,

Jacky shall have a new master.

He shall have but a penny a day,

Because he can't work any faster.'

'That's baby's stuff, i'nt it?'

'Not really. It's what you sing when you're on a seesaw, but when I hear kids singing that, I know they sing it without knowing what it means – just a song to move by, something to say, I suppose, because your body likes moving like that and you want to sing.'

Sadler closed his eyes. Very gently, he took Tom in his arms and began to kiss his face.

VI

A note on the table from Mrs Moore read: *Your lunch is in the oven – stew.* Sadler examined the careful round writing and thought wearily of the eternity of a Sunday that would follow this day. Mrs Moore, birdlike, would be singing to Jesus: he would eat beans and fart to break the silence.

Well, why think about it? Years ago he believed he had accepted loneliness, even used it well. His senses had sharpened, he had understood more than dreamed. Quite the reverse now. He fought it. He tried to smother it, curled up stupidly in the blanket of the past. The blanket made his skin itch and he scratched like a monkey. 'Just as well no one comes here any more,' he said aloud. 'Frighten the children I expect I would.'

'I don't mean to, of course,' he heard the Colonel say. 'I try to be gentle with the boy, but he'd run a mile rather than talk to me.'

The Colonel again. The Colonel standing awkwardly there in the kitchen, the hairs in his ears bristling. He'd come that evening to find Tom. He was going to shoot a rabbit or two, he said, and thought the boy might like to come along. But Tom had eaten his tea and run off.

'I was good with men, y'know Sadler,' the Colonel said dejectedly. 'But youngsters . . . I don't know . . .'

He'd gone off on his solitary shoot and returned an hour later with a smile and three dead rabbits.

'If there's one job turns my insides,' remarked Vera when she saw them, 'it's skinning poor little bunnies.'

Sadler considered eating some of the stew. The airing

132

he'd given himself seemed, now that he'd rested a little, to have strengthened him. But he still wasn't hungry. And anyway, if he could put off eating for an hour or two the afternoon would seem shorter. Nowadays he disliked afternoons. They reminded him that they were his 'free time' – the hours between half-past-two and half-past-four, when the Colonel dozed and Madge went round the garden with her secateurs – and 'free time' had no meaning any more. 'I'm all yours,' he used to tell Tom when Tom outlined, as he often did, some scheme – a new dam, a bonfire to build, 'but woe betide you if I'm late for serving tea. Don't know which'd be worse, Vera's moaning or the Colonel's fidgeting.'

In the summer Tom became an inquisitive rat, pink feet squelching up and down the river banks. Several times it got too dark to find his shoes. He'd come back with his shirt tied round his waist, telling Sadler that he should have stayed and never mind the Colonel's tea.

'Because it was great when the sun went. Some ducks came . . .'

But if he had the time Sadler followed him, the apprentice in river lore where Tom was master. And one afternoon, when Madge and the Colonel were in London and there was no tea to serve, they decided to walk fast, not stopping too long to look at things on the way, and go further up river than they'd ever been before. They walked for three hours. Tom mocked Sadler for being out of breath. Then they found the boats. They were tied to iron moorings, the property of a white painted pub. A neat notice informed the public that the landlord would rent out the boats at sixpence an hour.

'Cor!' said Tom. 'Could we?'

'Take a boat?'

'I got sixpence.'

'Then we could.'

Tom had learned to row on funfair lakes. Deftly, he put

the oar into the rowlock and steered the little boat out into the stream, his eyes as bright as the water. Sadler watched and revelled in his pleasure. Suspended on the quietly moving river, the green banks sliding past, he experienced such an absolute contentment that he tried to hold his breath, frightened that the least motion might shatter it.

'Wheee!' Tom laughed out. 'Watch me, Jack! Look, we're going ever so fast. Watch me!'

Well, he'd watched hadn't he? For five years, every movement, every grin, and passionately for every sign that Tom loved him. Now and then, Tom came to his bed, never guiltily, often oddly amused by Sadler's little rituals of passion, discovering his own sexuality with surprise and without emotion, then to fall asleep without a word while Sadler, tremblingly awake, held him. If he leaves me, Sadler thought then, what will be left? But each time that he'd held Tom he'd known that it would come soon enough, the parting. The war wouldn't last for ever.

And so one day it came.

Thirty-one Tom had said she was, Mrs Trent, Dolores, Dolly to all – Tom's Ma. She came driving down in a sports car one Sunday morning, a man at the wheel beside her, a Jack Flash of a man, shoulders padded, hair brilliantined, Charlie Ackroyd all over again. It was May 1945.

Madge was in the garden, going round in her linen hat, picking early roses, stooping before she picked to smell each one. She always chose roses for their scent, not for their colour or the arrangement of their petals. The scent of certain roses filled her with a sadness that she found exquisite.

'Just smell this, Sadler,' she called as she saw him cross the lawn towards her. 'Do just smell!'

Sadler bent to sniff the flower she was holding.

'Isn't that perfect, don't you think?'

'It's lovely, Mrs Bassett.'

134

'And now the war's over I can *believe* in the smell of a flower again, do you know what I mean?'

He did, he supposed. The funny things Madge said were occasionally rather pleasant. Looking up at her, he noticed that under the ridiculous hat she was pinker than her rouge.

Sadler cleared his throat.

'We've got visitors, Madam.'

'Oh?'

'Tom's mother and a gentleman friend.'

'Good lord!'

'Yes. Quite unexpected isn't it? She didn't even write after the first year.'

'What does she want, Sadler?'

'I didn't ask, Mrs Bassett. I imagine she wants to take Tom home.'

The Colonel was in London. As Madge took off her hat and patted her hair she thought how extraordinary it was that he always seemed to be away whenever something cropped up. Not that he, who had once handled his men so superbly, was very good at talking to people any more (in fact he didn't really talk, he growled), but he remembered for her all the things she wanted to say and had forgotten. And she knew that there was quite a lot that ought to be said to Tom's mother, if she could only think of it.

'What can I say, Sadler? I mean . . .'

'It depends why she's come, doesn't it?'

'Well, yes, but I do feel she ought to be reproached. I mean, it's terrible the way she's treated him, isn't it?'

'We don't know the circumstances, do we?'

Madge touched Sadler's arm.

'You're always so ready to be kind, Sadler aren't you? It's very nice. But there's no doubt in my mind that she's behaved very badly, very selfishly. I can't let Tom go without saying something, I really can't. I mean one owes it to Tom, don't you think?'

Madge handed Sadler her basket of roses as they crossed the lawn to the house.

'Shall I take your hat too, Madam?'

'Oh, my hat. Yes, would you? I look a fright in that don't I, but it does keep the sun out of my eyes. Now Sadler, tell me, what am I going to say?'

'Well, if I was you, Madam, I'd wait and see. There's two sides to most things, isn't there?'

To Madge's not particularly discerning eye there was only one side to Mrs Trent: she was a whore. Madge used the term loosely, of course, she didn't literally mean that the woman was 'on the streets' or wherever it was that these kind of people paraded themselves. What she meant really was that Mrs Trent was 'that type'. It seemed to be written not only over her face, but over each curve of her body, each tiny movement of her limbs.

She was standing by the drawing room mantelpiece, looking at the ornaments that stood on it. Her 'friend', hands in pockets, nudged her as Madge came in. Sadler, who had opened the door for Madge, heard her say nervously: 'Good morning, I'm Mrs Bassett.' He waited, listening, but this one remark seemed to be followed by silence.

Sadler went straight up to Tom. There was bright sunlight in his room coming through the thin, flowered curtain, but Tom still slept. Sadler sat down on a corner of the bed and looked at him. Tom was sixteen. His hair had grown darker. His body was still thin, but now it was strong. Sadler knew every part of it. He had kissed and caressed it, held it and penetrated it, believing that his love shaped its growing, that Tom needed him as much as he, released from what now seemed like years and years of death by this passion, needed the boy.

'Tom,' he whispered, 'my love.'

Tom turned over. He shielded his eyes from the sunlight with a hand and looked at Sadler.

'Did you bring some tea?' he asked.

Sadler shook his head.

'Why 'you staring at me, Jack?'

'Because I love you.'

'What's the matter though? You look all miserable.'

'Yes.'

'What'ser matter, Jack?'

Sadler walked to the window, drew the curtains and looked down at the orchard.

'Your Ma's here,' he said without turning.

'Go on!' Tom sat up and swung his legs out of bed.

'She is. She is here.'

'How d'you know it's my Ma?'

'She told me.'

Tom thought a moment, then laughed. '*She* wouldn't come!'

'She has come, Tom. She's got a man with her. He drove her down in his sports car.'

'What man?'

'I don't know. I think he said his name was Harrison.'

'It's no one she knew.'

Sadler turned. 'Well it doesn't matter, does it, Tom? The things that's . . .'

'You're always saying things don't matter.'

'I'm not, Tom, I was going to say what matters is . . .'

'Bleedin' Harrison. Could be anyone.'

'The man's not important.'

'Sez you, Jack. He is to me. It's my Ma!'

'Well, you'll soon discover who he is, won't you?'

'Yeah. But I don't like 'er turnin' up with just anyone. She's not like that, my Ma. She'd never go with just anyone.'

Sadler began to feel a rage inside him that distilled pain through his chest and arms and made him want to grab Tom and shake him and shake him till the boy howled. He knew that he had to control it because if there was to be a

137

parting it had to be gentle. Anger could have no place in a parting between him and Tom. He turned back to stare at the orchard, remembering how Annie had sometimes calmed herself by gazing, gazing without blinking at the trees outside her window. But the orchard couldn't help him now. Each moment was precious and yet his senses were being dulled by his anger. Never before could he remember wanting to hurt Tom.

'Tom —'

Sadler turned round but the boy wasn't there. Gone, of course. Eager to see his Ma, and why not? He loved her, still can love her. Sadler thought how Tom used to talk about her, slip her name in whenever he could. Then when she didn't write he never said anything, only stopped talking about her. Miserably, Sadler stared down at the apple trees. 'I never saw that in London,' Tom had once said of the orchard, 'trees are just green there, not all pink and stuff.'

Madge in the drawing room was feeling very hot after her walk in the sun. Her guests, after the first five minutes of shy silence, during which Madge made little sallies into brittle conversation, were now being very talkative. Scarcely listening to them, Madge was only conscious of the wet patches in her blouse under her arms and of her irritation that Geoffrey should have left her to endure this ordeal alone. 'I'm not good with people,' she'd once admitted to Sadler, 'I know I'm not. Some people of my — I mean, you know, like me, are terribly good at talking to everyone they meet. They can talk to people at bus stops, you know, or in the butchers. But I don't know why, I just can't get my right voice on. I seem to sound so stilted and awful . . .' She knew that when she did manage to say what she wanted to say now, her voice would make these people despise her. She wondered that she should mind, wondered *why* she should care at all, when she in her turn found them despicable. Their talk, this rambling perjury, it filled her with disgust. And the man Harrison, so smarmy, so cocksure; Madge didn't believe a word he said.

'Let me put it this way, Mrs Bassett. Let me put it another way. To be quite honest with you, we're not trying to make excuses. Dol – Mrs Trent isn't just rolling up like to claim 'er son without offering you something by way of an explanation. I mean ter say, it isn't as if we don't recognize that it must 'ave cost you a bit ter keep the kid. I said to 'er, we're going prepared to offer some remuneration. That's only right. I mean, she knows it's a long time, don't you, Dol?'

'Yes.'

'It *is* a long time. But that's been 'ard times an' all. Difficult for everyone, mind. I wouldn't deny that. But Dol's 'ad no 'ome, see? She was bombed. One of the first bombs ter hit London hit Dol's 'ouse. Sliced away 'alf her street. And if it 'adn't of been for friends she'd've been out in the gutter. Nowhere to go. All her things gone. So you see, she 'ad no home ter offer the kid, did she?'

Harrison stopped. Madge saw the two faces looking at her and thought wearily that the moment had probably come to say her piece.

'Whatever the reason,' she began, realizing as she spoke that she hadn't been listening properly, hadn't heard the reason, 'whatever the reason, I think it's pretty disgraceful that you can care so little for a child that you can leave him in a stranger's house for five years. Five years! Tom isn't a child any more. You deserted him, failed to provide a home for him during his most formative years.'

'But like I said, Mrs Bassett . . .' Harrison began.

'Don't interrupt me please,' said Madge, 'I owe it to Tom to say this to you. I think it's . . . I can't express what I think. All I can say is that you are lucky my husband isn't here because this whole business has made us both very angry indeed and ashamed, ashamed for Tom that you could so take advantage of the war to neglect your duty as a mother.'

'You didn't hear what he said, did you?' This from Mrs Trent.

'What do you mean?'

'He *told* you why I couldn't provide no 'ome for Tom. I didn't have no bleedin' home!'

'Why not?'

'Told yer she didn't listen. 'Cos it was bombed, love. Big bang crash – no more house!' Then piteously, 'I lost everything, see? Even lost me old cat.'

The sweat in Madge's armpits was ice cold. It was making her shiver. Such extremes of hot and cold, she thought, can't be good for my metabolism.

'I'm sorry,' she said. 'I'm sorry to hear that.'

'Well it was terrible, Mrs Bassett. If I were to tell you . . .'

'Yes, well I suppose you'd like to see Tom now, would you?'

'How is my Tommy?'

'Oh he's fine. He's been very happy here with us, after the first shock of moving. He's become very used to the kind of freedom he has here.'

'Growed up, is he?'

'Yes he is.'

'Well,' with a wink at Harrison, 'it'll be nice ter have another man about the house, won't it, Mick?'

Madge longed for them to go. She was feeling so weak that, quite empty of words, she walked as quickly as she could to the door and rang the bell for Sadler.

Vera heard Madge's buzz. She'd just sat down at the kitchen table to drink a cup of tea and have a glance at the *Daily Sketch*. Cursing, she got up to go and look for Sadler. It was going to be another of her bad days. Her ankles were playing her up, the Colonel had gone off to London just when she'd made him his favourite steak and kidney for lunch, and now Sadler wasn't down for his tea and Madam was buzzing for him. Wearily, she climbed the back stairs and began calling.

'Mr Sadler! Mr Sadler!'

Tom appeared on the landing above her, stuffing a clean white shirt into his trousers.

'Is she there, Vera?' he asked.

'What, duck?'

'Is she there? My Ma's come. Didn't you know?'

'No one told me, love. All I know is Madam's ringing for Mr Sadler.'

'No she's not. It's for me. She wants me to go down and see my Ma. Tell her I'm coming, Vera. Just got to get my shoes . . .'

He ran to the airing cupboard where his shoes, damp from a river outing, had been put to dry. Vera, out of breath as always when she climbed stairs, stood where she was. She couldn't bear any kind of confusion. Confusion immobilized her.

'I'm coming, Vera. I'm coming!' called Tom.

Then with his best jacket on he came flying past her, taking the stairs two at a time.

'Well, I don't know . . .' Vera muttered.

She turned and began to go down, then thought grudgingly, if I don't tell Mr Sadler tea's ready it'll be flippin' cold before he gets to it and then he'll be whining for another pot. So she trudged back up to the landing, called again, and getting no answer, trod quietly to Sadler's door. The door was open. She could see Sadler standing at the window, his hands pressed against the glass.

'Mr Sadler,' Vera said softly.

He jumped, turned towards her.

'What is it, Vera?'

She noticed that he was pale and his eyes were red.

''Ere,' she said, 'you all right?'

'Yes, I'm all right, Vera.'

'You don't look yourself, Mr Sadler.'

'I'm all right.'

'Tea's ready. Sure you're OK, dear? I could bring you up a cup.'

'No, no.'

'It's the news then upset you?'

'News?'

'Well, I just saw Tom. Said 'is Ma was here.'

'Yes.'

'Bit of a cheek, eh, after all that time?'

'Um.'

'Seem odd, won't it, if 'e goes?'

'Yes.'

'I think we've got quite fond of 'im, you an' I, though he is awkward. Remember when he first came, tiny little mite? Sat at the kitchen table all pale and scared to death. Now look at 'im!'

'Yes.'

'You're fond of him, aren't you, Mr Sadler? I can tell. You always had a soft spot for him, right from the start.'

'Yes, I'll miss him, Vera.'

'Oh well. Better fer him, I daresay. 'Ad to go back some time, didn't 'e?'

Sadler nodded. 'You go on down, Vera, and have your tea. I'll join you in a minute.'

When she'd gone, Sadler locked his door. Without making any sound at all, he wept.

Vera waited for him and Madge waited for him. Vera got up, put the cosy on the teapot, sat down again, thought how very used to Tom they'd all of them grown and so no wonder really if Mr Sadler wasn't himself. If the boy left, things would change. Tea-time for instance. She supposed they wouldn't really bother about tea any more. She'd make a jam sponge for Madam now and then, and brandy-

142

snaps for the Colonel if he asked for them, but all that bread and jam that Tom ate – at least a pot of jam a week – she wouldn't be putting that on the table any more. And it would seem strange to sit in the kitchen, just herself and Sadler, at five o'clock. There had been days, especially on winter afternoons, when Vera had felt that the three of them were very close. Even a bit, she sighed, like a family.

She heard Madge buzz again. More to protect Sadler than to demonstrate any eagerness to answer a summons, she untied her apron, stuck one or two loose pins back into her hair and went to the drawing room. When Madge's voice answered her little knock she went in.

'Oh it's you, Vera,' Madge said. 'Is Sadler out?'

'Must be, Madam,' lied Vera. 'I can't find him.'

Madge was sitting on one of the sofas, a cushion behind her head. There was no sign of Tom's Ma.

'Well, come in a minute, Vera. I'm feeling so upset, I would like just to talk to someone.'

'Certainly, Madam.'

'Sit down, will you?'

'Oh thank you.'

Vera perched, bony knees together, on the edge of a wide armchair that threatened each moment to engulf her in its padded comfort. She willed her body not to tilt.

'I don't know . . . I don't know why I should feel so upset,' Madge began. 'It's these people, Tom's mother and her . . . her man. I don't like to think of Tom going back to them. I feel I should try to stop him leaving, but what can I do? I've told Tom lots of times that he's welcome to stay. He's part of us all now. But I'm powerless, Vera. She's his mother and she has the right to take him back.'

'Well, like I said to Mr Sadler, 'e had to go back some time, didn't 'e?'

'I suggested they all went for a walk in the garden. Tom

143

came running down and then when he saw his mother he just stared at her and wouldn't speak. I thought the sunshine might help. I thought without me there they'd feel happier . . .'

Vera's ankles were sending shafts of pain up into her knees. She longed to sink back into the huge chair, put her feet on a stool and close her eyes. It'd be bloody nice, she thought, to stay 'ere just like that till all this Tom business is over and everyone, yours truly Vera included, starts to chirp up.

'Go on, dear,' said the Colonel.

'Well, as I was saying, it was all quite unexpected. I've never been so unprepared for anything in my life. I mean, down they come, without even a letter or a telephone call. It was as if it was all on the spur of the moment, you know, like deciding one day to go and buy a tortoise.'

The Colonel was very tired. Coming back from London on the train he'd dropped off, head lolling, mouth open, pushing out tight little breaths that smelled bad – a body in dissolution. Brandy poisoned him. He couldn't drink it any more and not feel half dead a few hours after. Each time this happened, he promised himself he wouldn't drink the stuff any more. But then there'd been one or two of his 'group' at the club; you had to have something after lunch if the group were there.

'Tortoise?'

'Oh you know what I mean, Geoffrey. I mean, why did they suddenly want Tom back now? I doubt they'd given him a thought in four years.'

'Working age, Madge.'

'What do you mean?'

'He's a wage-earner, dear.'

Madge stared blankly at the bits of the Colonel's face she could see through the candelabra.

'That's *awful*, Geoffrey.'

The Colonel shrugged. 'It's economics.'

'I never should have let him go! I felt it at the time. There was something in me which told me I should be standing up to those people, and for some reason I just couldn't. I didn't hear half of what the man was saying. If only you'd been there, Geoffrey . . .'

'What did he say?'

'Oh something about the Trent house being bombed. She tried to make that the excuse. She said she didn't have a home to give Tom.'

'Probably true. The East End had by far the worst of it.'

'Well, I know, but *she* must've found somewhere to live. She probably moved in with Morrison or whatever his name was. Why couldn't Tom have gone there?'

'Nuisance value.'

'Well, that's just it. That's just my point. They didn't give a damn about Tom. They just didn't care!'

Madge felt sick. Vera had made an excellent cheese soufflé, one of her favourite things, but now she couldn't eat it. She turned to Sadler who was standing behind her.

'I'm sorry, Sadler. I'm afraid I just can't eat tonight. Please tell Vera the soufflé was delicious – I'm just not hungry.'

'Yes, Madam.'

Sadler moved forward and took her plate away. Madge took a tiny sip of her white wine. The Colonel ate in silence for a while, then he wiped his mouth, nodded to Sadler that he had finished, and said to Madge:

'That was it, then?'

'What?'

'They just drove off with Tom?'

'Well, it seemed as if he wanted to go, didn't it Sadler? He was terribly excited. He couldn't speak at first, so I suggested they went out for a walk, it was such a lovely morning. And then while I was chatting to Vera, Tom came back and said was it all right if he went home now. And I thought, home, what on earth is home, Tom, when you've been here for so long? But he was quite casual about it – you know, the way he always is. It was as if he'd been working here for an hour or two, something like that, and was asking me if he could go.'

'Odd little chap.'

'What could I say, Geoffrey? I said as much I could. I asked him if he'd thought about it. I said, you're welcome to stay, Tom, if you want to.'

'Difficult for him.'

'But the real reason, you see, never occurred to me. I can't forgive myself for that. If I'd just understood why they were taking him back, I could have warned him, couldn't I? But I was so confused. And that's always my trouble. I'm always saying how important it is not to let people down and then I go and let them down without meaning to, without realizing what I'm doing.'

'Come on, old thing. You didn't let anybody down. I'd say you did what you could. We've been good to Tom. We've given him a home.'

'Well, it can't have been much of a home if he was so keen to leave it.'

'Well, that's only natural, I'd say.'

'If it hadn't been for Sadler, it wouldn't have been a home at all.'

'Sadler didn't mind, did you Sadler? You and Tom got on like thieves, didn't you?'

'Oh yes, Sir.'

'I'd say Sadler's the one to worry about, Madge, eh Sadler? Bet you're sorry to see the boy gone, what?'

'Well I am, Sir, yes. We've had some good times.'

'There, you see, Madge? Tom'll be all right. He'll learn a trade, I wouldn't wonder. Clever with his hands. He'll learn some kind of a trade.'

When Madge and the Colonel left the dining room,

Sadler snuffed the candles and cleared the table. He felt tired but he didn't want to go to his room. Sitting with Vera for an hour or two would be better than going there. He knew Tom despised him for being so sad because packing the boy's suitcase with him, sorting and lovingly folding his things, he'd looked up to find him staring angrily at him.

'Why can't you put them in, Jack? They're not the bleedin' crown jewels!'

He'd sat down on the bed and held out a hand to Tom.

'I'll miss you, Tom.'

'Well, yeah . . .'

'You can't imagine how much.'

'I'd've hated it here if it hadn't've been fer you.'

'I love you.'

'Well, yeah, in a way . . .'

'In every way. I love you terribly.'

Tom turned away. 'It's no good, all this. I can't spend my whole life like this!'

'Why not? I could get another kind of job and rent a place for us. We could —'

'Look, shut up, Jack. My Ma's waiting. I'll come back, won't I, an' see you? I always said I would. But I got to forget about all this an' go home.'

Sadler had kissed Tom before letting him go. He had pressed the boy's body against his own till he felt his resistance weaken a little and his mouth open. Parting from him then, wanting him and being given instead just the merest of smiles as Tom picked up his suitcase and left the room, gave him such pain that he stuffed his fist into his mouth to stop himself from screaming.

When Sadler went into the servants' hall, Vera was sitting on the grey couch, comfortable there with her knitting and comforted, after an upsetting day, by the familiar movements her fingers made. Only when she was following a very difficult pattern did Vera look at her knitting; usually she stared straight ahead, seeming not to notice what her hands were doing. She looked up and smiled at Sadler as he came in.

'Finished early in the dining room, didn't they?'

'Yes, I told you Mrs Bassett said she wasn't hungry.'

'Not my day, was it? Bleedin' steak and kidney lunchtime . . .'

'I'm sorry, Vera.'

'Not your fault, Mr Sadler. Just that kind of a day. Never mind, eh?'

Sadler took his pipe from the mantelpiece and began to fill it. It wasn't yet dark outside. The summer evening with its weight of scent hung there.

'Getting out, aren't they?' said Vera.

'What, Vera?'

'Evenings. Getting out.'

'Oh yes.'

'Nice time to be at the seaside, I wouldn't wonder. We went every year with my mum. End of May. We played battledore and shuttlecock on the sands. Whitsand Bay.'

'You should go back there one year, Vera. Take an early holiday.'

'Me? Oh lor no! Too old to paddle now.'

They both laughed. Sadler inhaled pipe smoke, thought how odd it was that Vera had a laugh twice her size. She stored up laughter, using it as she did so sparingly.

'Bet 'e'd never been ter the sea, 'ad he?'

'Tom?'

'Yes.'

'Only once, I think.'

'Told you, did 'e, his Ma took 'im?'

'No. I took him.'

Vera looked up at Sadler in surprise.

'Remember the evening last summer when I got back too late to serve dinner?'

'Do I!'

'We got a bus to Cromer.'

'You never said nothin'.'

'Tom wouldn't. He said he liked to keep things secret that he'd enjoyed. He said telling them spoiled them. We were late because the bus broke down. Tom enjoyed that more than Cromer.'

'Oh lor!'

'We all clambered out and sat on the verge, everyone grumbling. Tom found himself next to a fat woman with peeling shoulders and offered to pull the bits of skin off for her!'

'Cheeky little sod!'

'Oh she let him. Told him she couldn't reach. So he peeled each piece off and gave it to her. She just laughed and wobbled!'

'Well I never.'

'But he did like the sea, in a way.'

'The river was his favourite, wasn't it?'

Sadler nodded. No. He couldn't talk to Vera about that. He turned to look out of the window and Vera began counting her stitches.

'Twenty-two, twenty-four, twenty-six, twenty-eight, thirty . . .'

Sadler relit his pipe.

'Forty-four, forty-six, forty-eight, fifty, fifty-two. Well . . .'

'What, Vera?'

'Funny ter think 'e'll be back in London now. Bet 'e feels as if none of it ever 'appened.'

VII

Sadler was stirring the stew Mrs Moore had made for him at the beginning of the week. The meat was boiled to shreds and it looked repulsive, like sick. I'll give it to the dog, Sadler decided, but then he noticed that for what seemed like the first time in months, he was hungry.

He tried to imagine himself gobbling up the stew; sitting at the table with bowl and spoon, sloshing it down. What a sight! Hand so feeble it joggles the spoon, co-ordination gone, mouth gulps too soon and the boiled meat slides down the stubbly chin. But it would have to do. There was nothing else to eat – dog food and beans and bread, that was all. And the hunger was there, the first hunger for a long time. Or perhaps he had a worm to feed?

He sat down at the kitchen table and began to spoon up the stew. These days he'd listen to himself eating, *hear* the food going in, more than taste it. Funny that. Crunching biscuits deafened him. Senses all confused, of course; his body couldn't distinguish any more. Normal enough at his age.

He looked at the dog stretched out by the Aga, its back feet ridiculously crossed. It was making no sound at all that he could hear, so he stopped eating to listen for its little sighs of breath. But still nothing. No audible sound whatsoever. Sadler stared at it. Surely dogs didn't die with their legs crossed? He'd never watched a dog die. Perhaps, in their humility, they made no fuss at all, no final spasm or convulsion. Perhaps they always crossed their legs as a deception, so that their dying would give you no trouble. You'd just go to call them, those that had names, and the tails that always flickered with obedient delight in answer to your voice, would fail to move – and this your only clue.

'Boy!' Sadler used this term when it seemed necessary to call the dog something. 'Boy!'

But he could see now, not see, feel, *know* that the dog was dead and panic began to seize him.

'Dead, are you?' he asked, hushed. *'Are you?'*

The dog jumped, tried to get to its feet and fell over with a frustrated whimper. Sadler laughed with relief. You're going mad, old man, he told himself, fancy not being able to distinguish between life and death.

'All right,' he said to the dog, 'you can lie down again. I was only testing.'

He didn't love the dog. He didn't even like it very much, and yet the relief he felt that it was still alive didn't surprise him. With something like pleasure, he ate the rest of the stew.

And then, he thought, with a full belly I might lose an hour, if I'm lucky, sleeping. The Colonel always had a nap after lunch, but not until quite recently had Sadler remembered this, remembered that the Colonel would fall asleep seconds after his meal was finished, sometimes nodding off in his chair as he was brought his coffee. Madge said she knew it was unkind of her, she knew her husband loved his little sleep, but she couldn't help being irritated by it, day after day, that little bruise of irritation. It was, she seemed to feel, as if he was letting his body be rolled away down a steep hill. It was the loneliest moment of her day.

But there was no one left looking down if Sadler slept. He could snore all afternoon, wake up with the dark. But he had to choose. He couldn't, like the Colonel, sleep away night as well as day.

He began to search for his pipe. He thought it was on

151

top of the wireless, but it wasn't. So he started to go round the kitchen looking for it, opening cupboard after cupboard, staring blankly at things he hadn't used once since the day Madge and the Colonel died – silver and china and glass, all the paraphernalia of countless meals taken so graciously, so cleanly long ago in the dining room – then asking himself why he was looking there for something he used every day. He went back to his chair and sat down in disgust. 'Batty old fart! Clean round the bend, you are.'

Then he remembered seeing something in one of the cupboards that had interested him: a key hanging on a cup hook. And now he fancied he knew with absolute certainty that this was the key to his old room. But finding the cupboard again was like playing Pelmanism. Stiffly, he got up and began opening cupboard doors. Then the bell rang.

Shuffle, shuffle to the front door, but just before getting there, guessing he'd see the vicar standing on the step, and stopping, halfway across the hall, and shaking his head. Not now. Not the vicar now.

He waited motionless and the bell rang again. He had the feeling of wanting to hide. What if the vicar just opened the door and saw him standing there? He backed away, through into the stone passage that led to the kitchen, relieved when the door shut on him. But then he heard a car start up and the dog began to bark, and he knew it couldn't have been the Reverend Chapman because the Reverend Chapman always came on a bike and the dog never stirred himself for him. So out Sadler shuffled again, almost at a run this time, to crane out of the drawing room window. He saw a blue car, unrecognizable in its similarity to hundreds of other blue cars, disappearing down the drive, driven, he thought he could see, by a young man.

He cursed. The old foolish notion that his visitor might

have been Tom had unaccountably returned. He believed it long enough to feel dejected, and yet it was daft really when, for all he knew, Tom might be dead. Because he'd written hadn't he? All those years ago – the only love letter he'd ever written in the whole of his life – and not a word had ever answered it.

There'd been a day, just one in 1949, four years after Tom had gone back to his Ma in London, when the lad had borrowed a car – or stolen it – and come driving down, 'just to see you, Jack, because it's such a time isn't it, since we met, and I wanted you to see me now. Grown up, eh? Got me own suits now.'

The blond hair darker, almost brown, but still very thick; the smile studiedly crooked – Tom in his prime. And hours the smart young man had spent sitting with Madge, eating chocolates by her fire, even lunching with her and the Colonel in the dining room while Sadler served them. After the meal Sadler had gone straight to his room, knowing that Tom would come up to him. But it was almost half-past-three before he came – another hour and Sadler would have to be downstairs serving tea.

Sadler sat by the window and Tom lounged on the bed, talked about this job he had, selling cameras in a department store, talked about his Ma, married now, he said, and still in love enough to set the whole house rattling twice a week, talked and talked while the clock ticked on and all Sadler could do was remember the boy he'd held in his arms. Just after four, Tom said he ought to be going. He got off the bed and bent over Sadler and kissed his mouth. Sadler knew it was an insubstantial kiss, a gesture made for the sake of something past and ended, and yet at the same time he knew that if Tom touched him, he'd plead with him, beg to hold him just once more, humiliate himself, cry even, for the sake of the merest few moments.

But: 'No Jack, don't be soft. You were nice to me an' all that, and it was quite fun, what we did, wasn't it? But I'm grown up now. I'm not a kid no more. And I don't want all that pansy stuff. Pansies are creeps on the whole. Anyway, I fancy the other thing these days. It's much better, I'm telling yer.'

Sadler turned away, stared down at the orchard.

'Don't get all huffed, Jacko. Look I got to go now, got to get the car back by tonight.'

Sadler nodded.

'Come on, then, say ta-ta, won't you?'

'Bye, Tom.'

'Say you're glad I came.'

'Yes.'

'Cheers then. See you another time.'

That evening, Sadler began a letter to Tom. He asked him to change his mind. He ended it with a plea to let him spend his holiday with him, his two weeks of holiday, 'in some beautiful place away from this house and the demands of my work'. But the letter was never answered. He wrote again, just a note this time, telling Tom he was making plans to go to the Lake District. He'd heard about this little pub, not expensive at all, where you could stay and get breakfast and an evening meal. He said he'd heard it was very beautiful, the Lake District, and suggested that Tom bring his sketching things. He planned to go at the beginning of July, but while he waited for Tom's answer, Madge was taken ill.

She was bedridden for a month and Sadler's holiday came and went and he spent it calming the restlessness that the illness seemed to create in the other servants. Betty and Jane, both married, only worked part time now; they didn't belong any more and they were tired of Vera's grousing. Vera, whose soul ever seemed to crave excursions into caverns of total gloom, chose to believe that Madge was dying.

'Course, I blame the Colonel,' she declared, '*cherchez le homme*, as they say. 'E's never given 'er much love or nothing. Too wrapped up in himself.'

Over Madge's tray, Vera's thin, careful hands would hover for hours. With each meal she sent up, there'd be a flower in a tiny glass pot. But her heart, she said, wasn't in cooking for the Colonel. He'd never appreciated her food anyway, because, she explained, 'the army does that to you. Serve you up any old muck in the army. Ruin your palate.'

'Not to officers, Vera,' Sadler reminded her. 'Don't you remember Wren describing all those courses with different wines?'

'Same old muck – just more of it and dressed up like Sunday, that's all.'

So Vera decided the Colonel would eat what the servants ate. She was punishing him, she said, for 'neglect of a loving soul'.

A specialist from London was sent for when what had appeared to be a gastric attack had left Madge abnormally weak. He told her that she'd had a mild heart attack, prescribed a period of complete rest. 'Any exertions at all,' he cautioned, 'could cause another one that might be fatal.'

The idea that her heart was weak pitched Madge into a deep depression. She lay and studied her life. She lay and listened to the summer in her garden, thought how, in some people, those same sounds might have engendered thoughts of some significance, but in her nothing at all of any value, only a mild feeling of pleasure. She remembered summers when she was a girl, how hot weather had made her excited and that her mother had rebuked her for having red cheeks: 'It's so *common*, Margaret dear. Now go and lie down for half an hour. I want no one to see you like that.'

She'd imagined love then. She'd pictured herself decked out for love. She'd believed then, lying there as she lay now, that she could feel passion and that her adult life would be carried forward by passion. Supposing, then, there had been someone else, not Geoffrey, not the young officer she'd chosen at twenty-six. Who had she met in all those years until her marriage? No one. She could remember the arm – the same one or hundreds of different ones? – going round her waist, the nights and nights of dancing, but she could never remember any faces, never any eyes, mouths, that she might have kissed.

The Colonel came and sat with her. He read to her, and when she felt stronger, after two or three weeks, they played Gin Rummy. She'd always enjoyed cards, could become absorbed in a game in minutes. But she was terribly forgetful, no good at Bridge any more. The only games she remembered nowadays were Gin Rummy and Patience.

Over the cards she watched her husband. She longed to ask him where and how often in the years they'd spent together he'd found any love. Whenever she pictured him making love to anyone, it was always in the Savoy. And this thought would make her laugh. But she never asked him, because she knew he would have felt obliged to lie. He would never have understood that she hoped for his sake he had been unfaithful to her. He'd been her faithful companion – that was all she had asked.

The presence she found she liked best, as she lay there with her thoughts, was Sadler's. She'd tell him things. She told him that when she was eighteen, her father started to go mad. He began ferreting out ancient friends in London, and bringing them down to stay and offering Madge to them. 'There's my bond, there's my bond,' he'd intone, 'I give you my daughter!' The friends were embarrassed, couldn't even look at her, dressed as he always made her dress, in white. Some of them were married and began mumbling that their wives wouldn't like it and the old man would go into a rage which left him very weak and morbidly ashamed.

156

'I suppose,' Madge said, 'I must have been frightened of him. I know my mother was, but she was frightened of *rose petals* – she said they gave her asthma. I don't remember being frightened, only sorry. Someone had once told me that they shot dogs if they went mad, and I was afraid someone would shoot my father. He knew he was losing his grip on things, you see. He kept going to London to see more and more doctors. I went with him on one of the trips and in the train he took my hand and said he was sorry about offering me to his friends, he'd only meant it as a joke, as a sign of his affection. "But everything's got out of hand lately, Margaret," he said, "I don't want your mother to know, but I can't seem to get things straight any more." But I let him down, Sadler. He wanted me to be strong and help him and I cried. I cried in the train and he hit me to make me stop and there was a terrible rumpus in the carriage. He hardly spoke to me after that, hardly seemed to see me even.'

Madge sat up.

'I wonder,' she said suddenly, to banish her tears, 'if I'd had any children, what on earth they'd make of me?'

It seemed to revive her spirits to talk to him, to remember aloud. It was as if she were reading something she'd written long ago, long ago dismissed as trash, and then found herself surprised by how good it seemed to be. She *had* lived, she was trying to convince herself, there had been moments of joy and pain, odd flashes of understanding. 'The trouble with people like me,' she'd say, 'is we're too selfish. It's very difficult to feel compassion for selfish people.'

Sadler was still at the window, although the blue car had been gone some minutes. Perhaps, he now decided, it had been the vicar; it was like him to pay a visit just to show off his new car, if he had one. Somehow, the whole idea of vicars driving around in cars was amusing. The word of God passed, in Sadler's mind, only along a stretch

of dusty road where his Bible illustrator had drawn St
Paul, white-robed and barefooted on his way to Tarsus or
somewhere. The idea that the same message now toured
Britain in a Vauxhall Viva was hilarious, and Sadler
laughed.

Then he went upstairs, forgetting about the key he'd
been looking for, suddenly very tired and longing to sleep.
His room was neat, the bed made, the clothes put away,
everything tidy and very cold. He turned on the electric
fire and clambered into bed. In minutes he was asleep.

Waking, hearing the rain. Then walking downstairs,
aware of an unfamiliar voice coming from the servants'
hall. Stop and listen. The voice is familiar and yet the
name he tries to put to it won't come. Stand very still,
listening. The voice is deep, talks with extraordinary
smoothness. And then it comes. Of course: Richard Dimbleby.

Eight o'clock in the morning, but the servants' hall is in
total darkness, not a chink of light, only the blue flickering
screen and in the opposite corner the red pinprick that is
Vera's cigarette.

'It's a bit loud, Vera.'

'What, love?'

'The TV. Do you need it so loud?'

'Well, I don't want to miss nothing. Got ter 'ear it in the
kitchen.'

'You're not in the kitchen.'

'All right, dear, turn it down if you want to.'

Dimbleby's voice quietens, its smoothness now all the
more noticeable. The cameras make a jerky progress
down the Mall, glistening wet under wind buffeted trees, a
grey sheet of water between steep banks of hard seats, tier
upon tier of them. Vera shivers.

'Look at them, poor ducks.'

'Duck's the word, isn't it?'

Rows of people huddled in groups under umbrellas and groundsheets, wearing hats and macs of all description. An extraordinary sight. Countless hundreds of people sitting round-shouldered, staring at nothing, persecuted by the rain.

'And in June . . .' Vera comments, 'you'd have thought in June . . .'

The jolting image is gone. Now in the leaky shelter of wood and scaffolding, a family, white faced, stares out, caught by a roving camera, and one by one Mum and Dad and a couple of young lads bring out little flags to wave. The boys are bundled together in an old eiderdown, can hardly get their Union Jacks out from under it.

'Look at that,' says Vera. 'Been there all night, poor little mites.'

'The Colonel won't like the rain,' remarked Sadler.

'Oh lor!'

'Maybe they're protected, are they, the more expensive stands?'

'Like as not I'd say.'

'I wonder —'

'I know what you was going ter say, you wonder if we'll catch a glimpse of them.'

A cheer goes up. At last, for the waiting thousands something begins to move down the Mall, at last some meat for Dimbleby as a lone dust cart cleaning the route trundles into sight. The cheer passes from stand to stand as the cart makes its slow procession. Vera claps. The two men riding on the cart appear to acknowledge her with a grin.

Two hours at least before anything leaves the palace, thought Sadler, and in the meantime we'll watch the watchers. There'll be stories how this and that family have been camping for days to get a front row seat: 'I told the kiddies,' some rain-drenched Dad will announce to a rain-drenched BBC man, 'I said you'll come camping in the rain for a month if we tell you to. There'll be nothing like this again, not in my lifetime, maybe not in yours, who can say? What's discomfort, mate, compared to that? You won't see nothin' in life if you can't abide a bit of discomfort.'

Here in the house, they'll sit all day in the dark in the servants' hall. And Vera will do no more cooking on this day of days, can't bear to miss a minute.

'Won't you sit down, Mr Sadler?'

'Nothing to see yet, Vera.'

'You never know.'

'What about some breakfast?'

'Egg and bacon in the low oven, Mr Sadler.'

'Don't you want anything?'

'I've 'ad mine, duck. 'Alf past six.'

'You're daft!'

Sadler goes to the kitchen. The egg Vera has cooked is pale and solid, the bacon burned to brittleness. Vera never overdoes the egg or frizzles the bacon, but today, well, who can keep their minds on a job of work? Prudent, under the circumstances to have decreed a national holiday.

Sadler enjoys having the kitchen to himself, enjoys throwing away Vera's egg and frying himself some bread and tomatoes and making fresh coffee. He lingers over the little meal, and laughs, not so much at Vera, but because of the quiet pleasure he is feeling. When he wanders back into the servants' hall he is accused with a contemptuous sniff of having 'missed the guards'.

'What guards?'

'*The* guards. Look . . . we'll see them in a minute . . . look, there . . . all round that mound thing and down the Mall, see?'

'Do we have to sit in the dark, Vera?'

'Well, you can't see if you don't. It's like the pictures,

160

that's what the Colonel said when 'e showed me how to turn it on.'

'It was nice that they got a TV for us.'

'Well, we wouldn't like you to miss it, Madam said. I just couldn't bear to think we had the chance to see it and you didn't, that's what she said. Look, there's Mr Churchill arriving at the Abbey.'

'Is it? Now he looks his age, poor old boy, doesn't he? Looks a hundred.'

'Well, 'e is, isn't 'e? Not a hundred, mind . . .'

There is reverence now in Dimbleby's voice as the cameras follow the Prime Minister's shaky steps to the Abbey. In Parliament Square, as the rain keeps falling, people cheer him.

'Have you seen them yet, Vera?'

'Who, duck?'

'Madam and the Colonel.'

'No. Camera moves too fast.'

'Did they take mackintoshes?'

'Dunno. Shouldn't've thought so, not yesterday.'

'I hope they enjoy it.'

'We'll see more than what they will.'

'But we won't dance at the Savoy, Vera!'

'No. Never mind, eh.'

'Madam likes the Savoy. She often talks about it.'

'Who's that man?'

'Don't know. Never seen him.'

''E's gettin' a cheer.'

'They cheer everyone, they'll be hoarse by the time the Princess arrives.'

'The Queen, you mean.'

'She was looking forward to that.'

'What?'

'Mrs Bassett. They got me to book their table at the Savoy months ago.'

'Well, it's right to make a night of it. Come to think of it,

I could do with a beer meself.'

'Now?'

'Got ter start sometime.'

Sadler goes out to the pantry to get the beer the Colonel has ordered for them. When he returns, Vera is biting her gnarled fingers with delight and he sees that down the Mall the waving tip of the long ribbon of coaches has swung.

'Won't be long now.'

Sadler pours Vera a glass of beer and sits down. He reflects that the procession has a story-book flavour as it begins to gild the grey London street. A hand, these dancing characters seem to smile, opened the book and let us out and we'll prance for you, round and round, until the cheering has died and the umbrellas are folded. On and on, round and round, in all our magnificence until you close the book and we cease to exist. But our brightest jewel, the one we've saved almost till last, she gives our pageantry its wonder, because she is —

''Ere she comes!'

'And now . . .' Dimbleby is mellow with emotion, 'the moment these crowds, these thousands of people from all corners of the earth gathered here have waited hours, even days for . . .'

'God bless 'er!' says Vera, draining her glass of beer. 'That's what Vera says, Ma'am. God bless yer!'

Vera finishes her beer and then somewhere above Dimbleby's voice, above the bands and above the cheering, another noise claims attention, spoiling Vera's moment, pulling Sadler to his feet from the chair he is now comfortable in – the telephone ringing . . .

Sadler woke.

He was hot, his whole body damp with sweat, his mouth gasping for air like a fish, hands fighting their way up, grabbing the covers and throwing them back. But then, cold in seconds, in his own sweat, lying there freezing cold, remembering the dream and marvelling that, as always, the sequence was so exact, so free from the distortion dreams usually gave. And he could always stop it there, just as the Queen's golden coach began its ride to the Abbey and Vera drank a toast in beer and the telephone rang. He could always manage, at that point, to wake himself up – before he got to the study and lifted the telephone receiver.

'Hentswell Hall?'

'Yes, this is Hentswell Hall. Mr Sadler speaking.'

'Oh. Police here, Sir. Could you tell me please if you would be a relation of Colonel or Mrs Bassett?'

'No. I'm their butler.'

'I see. And there wouldn't be any relations staying at all in the house?'

'No. The Colonel and Mrs Bassett are . . . there's only myself and the cook.'

'I see. Well, I'm very sorry to have to give you bad news on this day above all, but I have to tell you that there was an accident early this morning involving Colonel and Mrs Bassett.'

'Accident?'

'Yes. Motor car crash. Colonel Bassett's car was in collision with a bus in the Knightsbridge area.'

Sadler sat down on the Colonel's leather writing chair.

'And the Colonel and —?'

'Bad news, I'm afraid. The hospital informed us that the Colonel died twenty minutes ago.'

'The Colonel's dead?'

'Yes.'

'And Mad — and Mrs Bassett?'

'She's in St George's, in Intensive Care. But they can't hold out much hope I understand.'

The image came to Sadler then: the Colonel and Madge, bizarrely coroneted like the peers and peeresses he'd seen going into the Abbey, riding side by side in an open coach, smiling as they waved. But then the coach began to weave and slide on the slippery road and the cheers that had greeted the smiling pair turned to shrieks of terror and people shouted out and began to point as one of the wheels went rolling away from the coach and it spun round and round like a fairground car, out of control, spinning and sliding and still they waved, Madge waved like a queen . . .

'You still there . . .?'

'Yes. I'm sorry, I . . .'

'If you would be kind enough to tell me who should be contacted. Sons or daughters?'

'No one. There's no one.'

'No children at all?'

'No.'

'Nephews or nieces? Someone of the family?'

'No. There's no family.'

'I see. Well, you will inf —'

'Should I come?'

'Sir?'

'To the hospital?'

'Entirely up to you. Everything, of course, is being done that can be done.'

Vera was at the study door.

'Come on, love. You're missing the best bit.'

Of course the Colonel never was very good at driving. Too used to Wren, Sadler supposed, learnt to drive too late. And London; he never could get on with traffic lights that looked three different ways. 'Far better, Geoffrey,' Madge had cautioned, 'to take a taxi from Knightsbridge Green. We'll never be able to park the car.' But, 'Nonsense, dear,' he'd said, 'just a question of leaving enough time.'

When the police telephoned again an hour or two later to say that Madge had died, all Sadler was able to recall was Vera's weeping, a thin, crouching, snivelling Vera, dabbing at her nose with a handkerchiefed paw, like a squirrel feeding itself nuts. Watching her, Sadler knew that she wept not so much out of sorrow, but out of fear. Such a rag of an old woman she was now, and never a very good cook at that. Vera had clung to Madge and her kitchen and her routine and, without her, she knew she was lost.

Sadler said nothing. An arm, he thought, laid gently round those hunched, heaving shoulders, might reassure, might be misinterpreted as guidance. But who was he to say to what hopelessness Vera had arrived? He just sat and watched her, till, empty of tears, she turned a clown's face towards him and said: 'let's 'ave the TV on again, Mr Sadler.'

He got up and turned on the switch and he and Vera sat side by side on the old sofa, waiting for the sound and the flickery picture. Then Dimbleby's voice, fallen unaccountably into what seemed like an imitation of Lawrence Olivier, clipped: 'The Queen is crowned. The Queen is crowned.'

BIG NIGHT FUN WENT ON INTO THE SMALL HOURS, so Madge's *Daily Mail* informed Sadler the next day. 'Princes, Ambassadors, statesmen and courtiers toasted the Queen in champagne and then danced until dawn at the Savoy.

'Beneath hundreds of yards of dove-grey material, which transformed the ballroom into a vast tent, set in an Elizabethan Garden laid out with camellias and box hedges, 1,200 of us feasted on foie gras, melon, sole, salmon and lamb.'

'So unfair of me,' Sadler heard Madge say. 'I'm always doing it, aren't I – telling you about things I've enjoyed. Very selfish of me, I suppose, but it was so wonderful. All those camelleias and little hedge sort of things and Noël Coward sang, all our favourites, you can't imagine, such a spirit of *Englishness*, so right, so moving, and of course that's what she said, wasn't it – "Let us cherish our own way of life." '

Well, for Madge that life was gone. The garden that had been her solace, that spoke to her, lulled her, would tilt a great green face towards the rain, never aware that she had existed.

Poor old thing. Yes, Sadler could think of her like that now that he was fully awake and not sweating any more and the dream had gone. And yet minutes ago – that dance of the open carriage on the wet street, wheeling, turning . . .

'Don't let her die, Ma,' he'd once said as *Little Dorrit* crept chillingly towards tragedy, and she'd only laughed. 'Nothing I can do, softy! It's in the book.'

Sadler closed his eyes. He had no idea if he'd slept for minutes or hours. He felt very tired, so he supposed he couldn't have been asleep for long, but he thought, time doesn't have the dimensions it used to, the ones I'd grown accustomed to. Somewhere, I've fallen out of step with time. Only lately. Part of madness, no doubt. The beginning of the humiliating end. He'd met old people (quite funny, they were) who never knew what day it was, Christmas or Tuesday, or what time of day, called everybody the wrong names, spat out every minute some morsel of a confused past. Death, their relations murmured, would be a blessed release from such embarrassing, even obscene muddling. Couldn't wait to bury the old things and put up clean white sensible stones.

The bed was wet. I'm worse than the dog, Sadler thought. At least he does it on the floor, not on his blanket. And now he had all the foul, tiring business of taking off the sheets, finding clean ones and putting them on. Did all old people piss in their beds? 'Never mind, Jacky,' his mother had said when he'd done it as a small child (too cold to get out of bed to use the pot, enjoyed doing it, feeling the heat creeping down his legs), 'you couldn't help it, love. And little boys always have more trouble than girls.'

Well, he certainly had trouble now. But he was too old to feel ashamed, much too used to living inside what he called his 'old wreck'. If it leaked, his feet got wet; too bad.

But then he thought, rather than tire myself out taking off the wet sheets, why not go and get that key and use my old room tonight? Up there, high above the orchard, he might sleep in the kind of healing, dreamless way he fancied he'd once slept. And seeing all the old things, the picture, the flowery curtains, the brass bed, might raise his spirits, help him to sort himself out. For of what importance to anyone or anything had been his last twenty years? Old already at fifty-three, tired already, so he'd believed, he'd been glad to shut himself away and let the world pass him by.

There had been Vera, of course, at first. Lonely, unlov-able Vera, whom he'd told to stay on if she wanted to, live like a queen in one of the best rooms if she wanted to.

'Lor! Don't seem right.'

'Why not, Vera? Everyone deserves a little rest, and now your turn's come along. It's a question of getting used to the idea, that's all.'

But she couldn't, she said, not live like *that*. So she'd gone on much as usual, living in her old room, getting up early to cook breakfast for herself and Sadler, until one morning she didn't get up at all, just couldn't move, she said, only her arms and her top half, the rest of her stiff as a ramrod and inert.

'Bleedin' 'eck, Mr Sadler, what's 'appened?'

She stared up at him from her pillow, her grey eyes popping with fear.

'Oh, it can't be anything, Vera. Just some odd thing. Your muscles have seized up after all that gardening you did yesterday.'

Because she had (and it wasn't like her) gone out that morning to do some weeding. The border was in a shocking state, she said, so she'd sallied forth, her stringy hair tied in a dishcloth turban, and with such a passion did her hands dig and root that by lunchtime the earth at the dahlias' feet was as clean as a hoovered rug, and Vera's cheeks were an undreamed-of pink.

'Blimey!'

Coming into the kitchen, wisps of hair escaping from the dishcloth, she looked, very briefly, quite young, younger than Sadler had ever seen her look.

'It suits you, Vera.'

'What does, duck?'

'Gardening.'

So it must have been that, he told her. She'd done too much, strained her back and legs with all that bending and kneeling. Whatever it was, she mustn't worry. He'd telephone the doctor and in the meantime, while they waited for him, Sadler would make breakfast and bring it to her.

'No. Nothing for me, Mr Sadler. Couldn't eat a thing.'

'You ought to, Vera.'

'No. No, I can't.'

And tears began to slide down her yellowy cheeks. She made no sound at all, no sobbing, no catching of breath, just lay there staring up at him while her tears rolled down her face.

The doctor came and went and came back when the ambulance arrived and Vera's matchstick body was carried downstairs wrapped in a red blanket. Because she would need proper nursing, the doctor said. It was too early to tell yet whether she'd ever get back the use . . . much too early . . . and the stroke was a very severe one . . . she must have absolute rest and quiet . . .

'Come an' see me, Mr Sadler, won't you? They forget

168

about you in 'ospitals, don't they?'

The doctor smiled.

'Of course they don't, Mrs Prinz, they —'

'Vera. You've got to tell everybody they must call me Vera.'

So. On his own after that. In his fifty-fifth year, still with a thick head of hair, grown rather long now that the Colonel wasn't there to remind him to have it cut. And with nothing to do but observe the little empty kingdom he ruled.

He often wondered how the Colonel would have filled his time, left on his own. But he found that he couldn't say, because it seemed that he'd never really known the Colonel, not as he'd known Madge, through all her little reminiscences. There had only been one occasion, one evening as Sadler was clearing the silver from the dining room table, leaving just the port decanter and one glass, when the Colonel had suddenly turned to him and said, 'I expect you think we lead jolly boring lives, don't you, Sadler?'

Madge had gone to bed. She hadn't been sleeping at all well, so she'd gone to bed early and taken a pill.

'Jolly dull lives, eh?'

'It's not for me to say, Sir.'

'Quite right, not for you to say. That's the kind of answer we expect from you, Sadler.'

There was a little wooden tray and a soft brush Sadler used to sweep the crumbs off the table. He began to walk round with it.

'Like port, Sadler?'

'I haven't often tried it, Sir.'

The Colonel lifted the decanter.

'Fetch a glass!'

'Are you sure, Sir?'

'Quite sure. Wouldn't have said that, otherwise. You get a glass and you can help me finish this lot.'

Sadler brought a glass and stood at the Colonel's elbow.

'Sit down. Go on.'

Sadler pulled out a chair, noticing, half ashamed, that his response to this odd invitation was a kind of dull tiredness. The room constrained him and made his body ache.

'Taylors '38.'

Sadler nodded.

'Go on then. Sniff a bit, then sip. Never gulp.'

'It's very nice, Sir.'

'Thought you'd like it. Trouble is, no one to drink it with these days. That's what happens when you get old, no friends – all gone. Much better to kick the bucket at sixty, let them all come to your funeral. Good health, then, Sadler!'

The Colonel raised his glass, drained it and filled it again. Sadler took another sip at his, found that the more he drank, the warmer the taste became.

'Cheers, Sir.'

'That's it. Thought you'd like it.'

It was 31 May 1953, two days before the Colonel died, and for once in his life he decided to say a few words about himself.

'. . . put it all down to loneliness, Sadler. I'm a stickler for convention, can't bear to live a day without keeping to the rules. If old Colonel Jarman I used to serve under walked in now, he'd say: "You're breaking a cardinal rule, Bassett, a cardinal rule." Know what that rule is?'

'No, Sir.'

'Never socialize except with equals. Never go up, never go down – cardinal rule. "Both lead to trouble, Bassett," old Jarman used to say. Bound to lead to trouble. But loneliness, old age – same thing – means you have to start breaking rules.'

'Are you lonely, Sir?'

'What? Lonely? Yes, I suppose I am. Bloody stupid of

me to admit it to you. All round the kitchen, anything I say, what? That's why I'm so damn careful. That and old Jarman. Never talk to anyone. Never say a thing. Always been a cardinal rule.'

'Very wise, Sir, I should think.'

'You know what they say – Prudence is the better part of . . . something or other. Valour, that's it, isn't it? Funny. Always used to think the wrong thing when anyone said that, used to think of a girl I once met called Prudence, used to imagine she'd gone off and married a chap called Valour or whatever it was. Better part – better half – you know? Damn silly. Can't think what made me think of that. Something to laugh about, I daresay. Don't find laughing too easy. Never did. I remember my school reports right back to prep school. "Takes himself very seriously" they used to say. "Takes himself very seriously" – damnfool thing to say about a boy.'

'Did you like school, Sir?'

'School? Enjoyed Eton. Eton was the making of me, you know that, Sadler? Not that there was a great deal to make, eh? But it taught me the cardinal rules – Eton and the Army. You get a lot of people these days saying they don't like rules, all panting to do what they like, any old way. But that's not right, not in my view, old-fashioned and all that. No fun shooting tame ducks, eh?'

The Colonel smiled. He didn't often.

'Talking too much, aren't I? But I don't suppose you mind. I expect you've often said to yourself, I wonder what goes on in the old fool's head? I wonder what he thinks about with all that time on his hands? Haven't you?'

'I always wonder about people, Sir. It's part of my job to try to find out how people think, then I know what pleases them.'

'Damn good answer, Sadler. You're a bright chap, Madge always said so. I daresay you'd have done all right

171

in business.'

'Oh I never had that kind of brain.'

'But you're quick, Sadler. That's what I looked for in my men, quickness.'

'Oh it's just some knack I've learnt. I once worked for a butler called Mr Knightley. He made me learn the importance of quick answers.'

'Lot of mumbo-jumbo most of the time, I suppose? Yes Sir, no Sir, three bags full Sir. Get on your nerves, does it?

'No.'

'It's quite right, of course. The guardians of graciousness, people like you; that's a phrase I thought up years ago at a house party and I thought it was so apt, I kept on using it. Even wrote it down, I think. Have to write everything down. Always did. Even wrote a memo to meself to ask my wife to marry me! Damn silly, eh? Especially when she was so bloody pretty. Margaret Kenyon. Prettiest thing I'd ever seen.'

He paused, took a long sip of his port.

'Never forget it. Met her at a house party someone had given. Spent the whole weekend trussed up in my lieutenant's uniform. Far too hot, should have been wearing white flannels, but she said she loved the army, said she thought uniforms were whizzo, or whatever it was we used to say then. So I kept it on, just for the pleasure of having her look at me. And then do you know what she said when I left? Said she'd changed her mind about uniforms, thought they were horrid things if they made people so hot and uncomfortable! Serve me bloody right, eh? Conceited young dog. "Takes himself very seriously" – quite right, what?'

Sadler smiled.

'Can't imagine why I should tell you that, Sadler, except that it's damn nice to remember things out loud for a change. That's what old age brings y'know, memory. Curse it sometimes, wish I couldn't remember a damn thing. Give anything just to have a blank. Not possible, though. Just not possible. That's all you are when you get old, Sadler, an old windbag stuffed with the past. Jolly good past, though. No regrets. That's what a contented man ought to say, isn't it? Come on Sadler, never let the glass get more than half empty – cardinal rule.'

Sadler held out his glass and the Colonel filled it.

'Tell you what, though. I married a wonderful woman and I've never tolerated a word said against her, not in my presence, but I used to do a bit of rampaging – a man's right in my view – and I broke a rule, Sadler, only once, mind, but nevertheless I did. I broke a cardinal rule and let everything get out of hand, just that once, couldn't help meself, fell head over heels.

'You see, you'd never have dreamt it, would you? What a boring life the old buffer has, you said to yourself, didn't you? No excitement, eh? Well, it was only once, mind, the year before you came, the year before the War began. And what a lady! Never knew the slightest thing about her, except that she was fond of gymnastics. Picked her up in Kensington Gardens, but nobody could infer from that that she wasn't a lady. Years younger than me, of course. Years and years, and what a goer! She never stopped, Sadler, and I just used to lie there and marvel at her, marvel at meself too, never knew I had it in me. And of course it made me so bloody happy, I couldn't leave her, Sadler. I couldn't let go. Always had been able to let go before, when I was young, abroad you know and all that, but this time I couldn't. Don't know what it was about that girl. Do you know she could turn a cartwheel on the window sill? Bloody marvellous, eh? Cartwheel on the window sill. I used to make her do it over and over again until she was dizzy.'

Sadler laughed.

'Funny, eh? Yes, I suppose it is really. I was funny to her, I expect. Probably said, silly old buffer, probably had

173

dozens of young chaps queueing up. But she'd never take money. Never took sixpence from me, not that type at all. A present now and then, of course, some little thing I'd bring her, but never money. Angela, her name was. I used to call her my angel.'

'Do you still see her, Sir?'

'Me? No. She got tired of me. Much too old for her. Not surprising. Much too old. Can't think why I'm telling you this, Sadler. Probably because it was so important to me. I was in love, Sadler, hook, line and sinker. I used to say to myself, I'm in love with an angel. Damn silly, really. Thing was, I couldn't let her go. I couldn't say to meself, Geoffrey Bassett, you are never going to see your angel again. I just couldn't do it. And that's the rule I broke, Sadler. Never pester, never put yourself where you're not wanted any more. But that's exactly what I did; I pestered and pestered her because I said to myself, it's the last time, I'm much too old for it to happen again, much too old for love and all that business, to do it properly. But I could with her, you see. She *made* me do it. I'd only got to see her. I'd only got to say: "Angel, what about a cartwheel . . .?" '

'She got married, did she?'

'What? Oh yes. So she said. Going to marry an American, so she said. Nice young American, good at baseball. Good for you, Angel, I said, but she knew I didn't mean it, knew I'd go on pestering her till she threw me out one day. Suppose it was all she could do. I was such a damn nuisance.'

Sadler nodded. Sipping port like that, he and the Colonel might have been old friends.

'Never wanted to get married, Sadler?'

'Me, Sir?'

'Yes. Never thought of trying it?'

'No. I'm really very content, Sir, stuck in my ways, too.'

'Lots of tomfoolery talked about marriage.'

'Yes.'

'Damn right. A lot of tomfoolery. Mine's been happy, mind, even though I muffed it where it mattered. I muffed it – not Margaret's fault. She knew what it was all about, said she'd imagined it thousands of times, her "wedding night". Thousands of times, eh? Women are bloody marvellous sometimes, aren't they? Full of romantic dreaming. Funny thing is, nothing seems to disillusion them. But I muffed it all right. Drank too much. Too bloody nervous; Margaret Kenyon, I thought. Margaret Kenyon – my wife! But I never imagined we'd have to go our own ways like we did. I wanted her all right because she was a marvel, Sadler. I could find a picture of her that's better than Garbo! Bloody marvellous looker, my Madge was. Kept sheltered, of course. Neurotic mother, father in a looney bin – or should have been. Never forget going and asking the old man if I could marry Margaret. He was walking in the orchard, in a tailcoat and no shoes. Barmy! And d'you know what he said to me? "I know what you've come for," he said, "you've come to confess, haven't you? How was it, then? Was it satisfactory? Did you take her from behind when she wasn't expecting it? She's a smart one, my Margaret, don't try and tell me you caught her unawares!" Mad as a hatter, Sadler, impossible to communicate with. So I thought, fine, old chap, I'll play your game, if that's they way you want it. So I told him I very much enjoyed going to bed with his daughter. "I enjoyed it very much," I said, "so did Margaret. Now we're going to get married." But that narked him, you see. "Taking her away, are you?" he said. "Can't do that, young man. No one takes my daughter away from me!"

'They took him away, poor old boy. Quite right, of course, dreadful liability. But then again, he was quite lucid some of the time, knew just what was going on and said he didn't like the idea of being locked up. I felt sorry for him. Madge used to be very distressed. But going to see him wasn't any good. We tried, of course. Several times. He'd talk to me all right, very friendly even, but he wouldn't say a word to Madge, never would say a single word to her. Some incident on a train, or something. Never did find out. But he never talked to her after that – tried to pretend she wasn't there. How's your glass?'

'I'm doing fine, Sir, thank you.'

'Being boring, am I? Expect I am. Never could tell a story like Jarman could. He had a knack. Old Jarman even made you laugh when he couldn't remember the ending. Well, so you like a good port, do you, Sadler? Does your heart good – in moderation. Everything in moderation, another cardinal rule. Drank too much when I was young, of course. Champagne was the thing, not so expensive as it is now. I taught Margaret to like champagne, always thought it might help us in bed. Couldn't have been more wrong. Terrible business. The saddest thing of my life. Just couldn't make it, Sadler, not with my wife. All right with anyone else, but not with the woman I loved. Ghastly business. But she never mocked me. Never once in her dear sweet life did she say an unkind thing. She's loved me all that time, Sadler. She's been my life's companion, all these years, and I never once satisfied her. Sometimes I ask meself, how can you hold up your head and look at her? How can you bear it?'

Sadler granted the Colonel the silence for which, the following day, the old man would undoubtedly be grateful. It was getting dark in the room and both of them were thankful in a way for the dark. A minute or two passed and then the Colonel suddenly said, 'Better go and take me trousers off. Bloody wet meself.'

VIII

Sadler dozed again. When he woke the room was full of orange light. Sunset. For a moment he couldn't remember if it was summer or winter, if the sun going down meant night or only mid-afternoon. He lay still and stared at the windows. The sky was marvellous, a real charcoal fire of a sky. 'Last!' he said to the sunset, 'go on, last!' Less than half-an-hour, though, and it was gone and the room quite dark.

His body in the saturated bed felt cold and weak, and there was cold sweat on his lip. He wanted to call someone. A face, arriving at his bedside, a hand to hold his that felt so limp and useless – if only he could have called out for that. Mrs Moore would have done. Anyone would have done. And a cup of tea. He would have asked for a cup of tea and sat in the armchair drinking it, while the sheets on his bed were changed.

There was a bell dangling above his bed. Downstairs, outside the kitchen, a red disc marked *Bed. 2* inside a glass case was set jiggering when you pressed it, so that the servants would know which room to run to. Sadler reached up and pressed the bell and he heard the dog begin to bark.

Vera was all right, he thought, in a hospital. In hospital, there was always someone to answer when you rang a bell. Vera's own special nurse had wide, freckled arms, and when Vera wanted to shit, those arms would lift her as easily as they might have lifted a child and hold her firmly as she sat on the pan.

'You know, Mr Sadler,' Vera had said once when he visited her, 'I'd always 'ave said it'd be 'umiliating, all that carry on, but they sense it, you see, nurses sense how you're feeling.'

'She seems nice, that nurse, Vera.'

'Oh she's lovely, i'nt she? I don't know what I'd do without kindness, Mr Sadler. You were always kind to me, and now 'ere . . .'

She cried so easily. She cried every time he went to see her. He'd sit in the chair and Vera would lie there crying, not even bothering to wipe away the tears.

'Come on, Vera dear. You're taken care of. And what about that tingling you had in your leg the other day? That was a good sign, wasn't it?'

'Didn't feel it no more. Think I imagined it.'

'You don't imagine things like that.'

'Well I do.'

But she had been cared for. That ward of hers had been a bit crowded and it was so hard to sleep, she complained, in that line of wheezing, snoring old ladies, that they had to give her sleeping pills, and that depressed her. The recipe for a good night's sleep, she'd always said, was to get up early, and so no wonder, because now she never got up at all.

'Remember those mornings, doin' Madam's tray?'

'Never forget them, Vera, the care you took.'

'Little sprigs of parsley on 'er butter.'

'Clean tray cloth every day.'

'She knew I took trouble.'

'Of course she did.'

'Poor old thing.'

Then the tears again. Nodding there on her pillow, her eyes brimming over. Sometimes her freckled nurse would pass and see her crying and come and puff up her pillows and try to think of a joke to crack. Sometimes Vera clung to her arm.

178

Yes, they'd cared for her, as far as they could. They hoped she'd die, because they knew she'd have to lie there till she did.

No, thought Sadler, whatever was I saying – Vera was all right? She wasn't all right. She'd lain there for nearly two years, staring out at the long ward. She'd seen people die in beds that were occupied by other people the next day, seen them die and so on and on, until she was the only one left of the original company. Then she died in the night, in her sleep, drugged no doubt, and unaware. Sadler had gone to visit her the following day and found someone else in her bed. She'd been replaced.

No one to replace me, thank God, he thought. He'd seen to that. Left the old neglected house to the state, left it all to the Government, because at least they'd think of something sensible to do with it. They'd see it was filled with pregnant women, or geriatrics, and it would flower, its windows would shine with usefulness, and the infants born there or the old people dying there would, for a day or two, fill their lungs with the air of paradise – for wasn't it paradise that the place had once been called? And that view from his room, that sky of a moment ago, that was as good a first or last glimpse of God's heaven as you were likely to get. You couldn't grumble, if, through eyes half open or eyes almost closed you saw that.

Dreadful, though, to start counting sunsets. A hundred more? Ten more? Only one more? Or couldn't you be certain even of one? At his age and with this coldness and this feeling of not wanting to move . . .

Get up. That was it. Get down to the warm kitchen, have a word with the dog, make tea. You'll feel better if you just get up and dress and get into the warm. You could listen to the wireless and in no time you'll have forgotten Vera and all this maudlin nonsense about sunsets. And then after tea, you could look for that key again and spend the evening rummaging about upstairs in the room, seeing

179

what's there, getting absorbed, forgetting to notice time, go to bed late in that narrow bed, sleep through Sunday, sleep without dreaming till it's Monday again and Mrs Moore comes . . .

Sadler was going through all this in his mind, but he hadn't moved. Moving seemed so difficult, his body so sluggish. Downstairs the dog was whining. Tired of the hot kitchen, probably, dying to get out and sniff the dark.

'Coming!' Sadler shouted. But still he didn't move. I could, he thought, if I just had someone to hold on to, to get me started. If I just had Mrs Moore's skinny arm, or Vera's nurse's big freckled one. If someone could just help me to sit up, I'd be all right. I could get my legs going then, swing them out even. Because it wasn't as if he didn't have a reason for getting up. Thousands of times, he must have got out of bed to stare at a blank day, days and days empty of purpose and meaning. But today, he'd had this brain-wave about visiting his old room, and he wanted to go up there, he was looking forward to it. He kept imagining how he'd feel as he walked in. He *knew* it would make him feel better. So why, when for once he had something to do, couldn't he move?

He put his arms behind his head, raising it up, so that he could watch the gathering darkness more easily. And he thought about lying just like that in a little flat bottomed boat on a hot afternoon, watching the mayfly hatching off the water, lying absolutely still, trapped by the heat, lulled by the sound of the water licking the boat, letting his eyes move now and then, but nothing else, only his eyes moving lazily from the shining water to gaze up at Tom's face that was pink from the effort of rowing and that now and then smiled at him. That was a stillness he hadn't wanted to break. It was so perfect a stillness that he hadn't even dared to move a muscle. Thirty years ago now. Thirty years since he'd loved.

He heard an owl hoot and it made him smile. Because

for a long time he'd pretended to be frightened of owls, told Annie that their hooting scared him, so that she'd come closer to him. They hadn't really frightened him at all, or if they had, he'd soon forgotten it. Owls were just an excuse to make Annie stroke his hair, to drift softly to sleep held in her arm. It was beyond imagining now, that kind of peace.

Carefully, Sadler brought his arms down from under his head. They'd only been there a minute or two and they were stiff already. Then, pushing back the bed clothes, he levered himself up on to his elbows, pushed himself back till he was sitting propped against the bedhead. He reached out and turned on the light. The light was blinding. He sat still and blinked until his eyes were used to it. Then he stared at the room. It was such an empty room, almost nothing in it; just the bed, a bedside table and lamp, an armchair and an electric fire. 'Can't abide clutter,' the Colonel had said, stroking his cupboards. 'Clutter's for women. I like empty space.' But open any one of the cupboards and what would you find but the clutter of ages, the debris of a whole life. And somewhere, among all those discarded things, there was a lock of hair perhaps, or a photograph of a girl he'd called Angel. Just shows, thought Sadler.

It was easier now, with the light on, to get out of bed. He managed it without any pain at all, but his body stank of urine; he'd have to wash that away at least, even if he did nothing about the bed. So he put on his dressing-gown and limped off to the bathroom. He ran some hot water, took off all his clothes and began to sponge his body.

He never looked at himself any more, only at his chin when he remembered to shave it, but never at his body. The sight of it disgusted him. Not that, as a young man, he'd been particularly proud of it. It had been straight enough and quite strong, but nothing you'd want to show off. No, what he would have liked was to be a child, to be the boy he once was. There was a photograph of himself, just the one (taken by the treacherous Betsy), of him and Annie hand in hand. He still had it. Sometimes he'd sit down and stare at it with a magnifying glass, trying to see in that tiny face some connexion, some unalterable relationship with his own. And there was nothing.

Cleaned with soap, at least his body was less repulsive than stinking of itself. Sadler allowed himself the briefest glance at it before he brought it back to the camouflage of its old clothes. He sat down on the bed to put on his socks and the smell of the sheets made him retch. To think that a moment ago he'd been lying there . . .

'Smells of piss, this 'ospital, Mr Sadler.'

'No. It's only ether, Vera. They all smell of it.'

'This one smells o' piss.'

'Look, smell these flowers, dear.'

Chrysanthemums. They hardly smelt at all.

'Oh lovely.'

Sadler was dressed now and about to go downstairs. Then he heard the car. With his bedroom light on, betraying his presence, there was no hiding this time from his caller. When he heard the car door bang, he went to one of the windows, trying to see through the reflected room into the darkness beyond. He craned and squinted, but he could see nothing. The lights of the car were turned off. Then the door bell rang and the dog, bristling to his role as guard, trotted out into the hall and began a defiant yapping.

Sadler shuffled out on to the landing and looked down. He could see the dog and he could see the front door, but neither gave him any clue. But he'd have to open the door. Too late now to turn his light off and play dumb, and there was no one else (not like in the Colonel's day) no one else to send. He's got me, Sadler thought wearily. Could be death itself, and I'd trot obediently to the door, open it with a smile.

'I'm coming!' Sadler called.

Seeing him come down the stairs, the dog ceased its yapping, looked expectantly from him to the door.

'Good boy,' said Sadler.

Sadler opened the front door, brought his eyes cautiously round it.

'Only me.'

'Who?'

It was so dark outside with the light gone in the porch, that Sadler could only see the white of a face, not a face he knew.

'Me. Can I come in?'

The Reverend Chapman was a stubby, rather unkempt man. Just right for the small part of Barrabas he'd played in a crucifixion play at school. His hair, once very thick and black, was thinning; his skin, which looked as if it should be tanned, was yellow. His hands seemed, year by year, to get larger and more clumsy, or his Bible smaller. He wasn't what you expected a vicar to be.

'I called earlier.'

'Did you? That was you, then?'

The dog, his tiny burst of aggression spent, was all friendly docility now. He came a-licking, and the vicar, always trying for the appropriate gesture, bent down and gave him a pat.

'Silly to say, not disturbing you? Bet I am. I usually am. People are too polite, thank the Lord, to send me away.'

'No, you come in Mr Chapman. It's a change for me to have a visitor. Tea?'

'Yes, thank you. If it's no trouble.'

'Come in the kitchen. It's warm in there.'

The vicar looked about him.

'It's a long time since I was up here.'

'To tell the truth, I don't remember. Don't make much sense out of time these days.'

183

'Living alone, Mr Sadler. None of us is very good at living alone.'

'Well I'm good at it, done it for long enough.'

'Get about much these days, do you?'

'Oh I totter. The dog's as bad as I am, both of us old.'

'I remember you had a dog. What was it you call him?'

'Nothing. No need.'

The vicar sat there nodding, while Sadler made the tea. When he turned round he saw beads of sweat on the vicar's head.

'Too warm for you?'

'Well, it is warm, yes. I'll take my coat off, that'd be better.'

'Feel the cold myself.'

'Do you?'

'In the joints.'

'Oh yes.'

'I'm seventy-six any time now – today even.'

'Same age as the year.'

'That's it. Born in 1900.'

'Oh.'

'Sugar, do you?'

'Well, I do. Except in Lent.'

'One spoonful or . . .?'

'No, no, none, Mr Sadler. It is Lent.'

'Is it? Forty day and forty nights. Surest way to beat the devil is to grow old. Nothing to tempt you when you're old.'

'Very probable. But we all have our little indulgences, even in old age, don't we?'

Sadler chuckled. 'Nothing much left to indulge!'

The vicar nodded. He ran his hand through the strands of hair that crossed his bald patch. Without realizing it, he left a few of them sticking out. Then he took one nervous sip at the tea Sadler had poured for him and cleared his throat.

'I saw Mrs Moore in town today.'

'Did you? Well, she still comes and does the chores.'

'I would have called on you, anyway, I daresay. I like to get round all my parishioners from time to time. But I came mainly at her insistence.'

'Drink your tea, Mr Chapman.'

'Oh, I will yes. Well, you see she does feel —'

'Ssh, boy!' (To the dog who had begun for no reason to whine.)

'She feels that things aren't right here, Mr Sadler.'

'Oh yes?'

'She couldn't explain —'

'Quiet now, boy!'

'And normally, I never like to intrude, not where I'm not wanted. But a man's soul lives in a wilderness, that's how I imagine it, a thirsty wilderness, and I like to see the Church as a clear running stream . . .'

Sadler smacked the dog's nose; it turned a cowering little circle and lay down at his feet.

'As a what?'

'As a stream, clear running and —'

'Seen the stream, have you?'

The vicar shook his head.

'It used to be a nice place to go, but it's full of muck now. The boy used to build these dams.'

The vicar examined Sadler's face, and found that it disgusted him. Repulsive old man, he thought, let God punish him.

'Yes, we used to have fun down in the stream. If it wasn't so dark and I wasn't . . . I could take you and show you.'

'Another day, perhaps.'

'The first row's the difficult one. You must get really big stones for your foundations, or you never get started. But we mastered that little stream; we could have flooded the meadow.'

'Well, as I —'

'You've got a car, then, Vicar?'

'A car? Oh yes. I've had that some time.'

'Saves your feet, does it?'

'Yes.'

The vicar ran a hand through his scant hair again.

'Well . . .'

'You'd like to be getting along?'

'Oh no. I stay as long as I'm welcome. I try not to intrude, but I'm not a travelling salesman. I come to everyone, not just the good clients.'

Sadler's head ached. He wanted the vicar to leave.

'I'm one of your worst, I daresay.'

'You're very courteous, Mr Sadler. God will de —'

'Mrs Moore makes up for me, doesn't she?'

'God will judge. But I'm happy you mentioned Mrs Moore again; I'm afraid I —'

'She prays for me, you know.'

'I believe she does.'

'It's not enough, of course.'

'I might as well tell you, I told you a bit of a lie just now.'

'You, Vicar? God wouldn't like —'

'Yes, it's always in circumstances like this, a very delicate choice between constructing a story and giving pain. I don't like to see pain, Mr Sadler, and I see it every day. Sometimes I feel I can perceive pain where others see none, nothing at all . . .'

Sadler put down his teacup.

'I'm puzzling you, aren't I? Very wrong of me. I should tell you what I came to tell you and I will.'

'Quiet, boy!' Sadler kicked out at the dog, whose whining hadn't ceased.

'It concerns Mrs Moore. I lied when I said I met her in town. She telephoned me this morning and asked me to talk to you then, before she left, but I believe you were out and couldn't come to the telephone. She found it difficult

186

to explain things to me. She said she didn't want to let you down, Mr Sadler, but she'd been trying to tell you for weeks and she didn't know where to turn, but to me. You see, she's a nervous woman, not terribly well, and for a long time now, months, I think, she's been finding it very distressing to work here. She couldn't really tell me why, but she made me realize what a burden this work was for her. She wanted me to tell you that she won't be coming any more.'

'Too untidy, am I?' Sadler's voice was very flat.

'No, no, I don't think so. But it's a big house, isn't it, and she's not young any more. And I think she'd like more time to herself and more time for God.'

'I never used to be untidy.'

'You must understand she didn't want to let you down. She told me she asked you some time ago to find a replacement.'

'In the Colonel's day, there was never any dust here. I supervised all the cleaning. And there was a lot of furniture in those days. Most of it sold, now, you see . . .'

'No, it wasn't that, Mr Sadler. She had no complaints . . . she couldn't pin it down. But I could see pain. I could see pain without seeing her. And I knew she needed my . . . interception.'

The dog skulked off to its mat by the Aga. With a bright black eye, it watched Sadler and a series of little tuneless whimpers escaped from its body. Sadler thought suddenly, I love the little rat. He thought he would have felt comforted if he could have lifted up the dog and held it close to him. And he felt ashamed that he'd never given it a name.

'Well . .'

'You going, Vicar?'

'I'm the bearer of bad tidings, am I? I'm sorry, I didn't know you relied so much . . .'

Rover, Fido, Rex . . . those were dogs' names, weren't they?

'There's a good delivery service, I suppose, for your groceries?'

But named, the dog would take on too much importance, become indispensable to him and he couldn't let that happen.

'Mather's deliver still, do they?'

Sandy, Bonzo, Scamp . . . No. Better to get rid of the dog now, quickly before the name came to him.

'Mr Sadler . . .?'

No need, in this freezing weather, to have him put down. Just shut him out one night, bury him in the morning.

'I must be going, Mr Sadler.'

He must do it soon, or the name would come to him.

'I'll leave you then. Got to make a few more calls tonight. Never any time on Sunday, not now I cover three parishes. Musical pulpits, a vicar's life is these days!'

Sadler just nodded.

'I'll pop in again, soon.'

Sadler didn't stir. Not even to take the hand proffered to him.

'No chance of seeing you at matins in the morning?'

Sadler shook his head.

'Another time perhaps. Well, I'll see myself out.'

And so he was gone. Sadler sat still, waiting till he heard the car start up and drive away, and then he shut his eyes, listening very very carefully to the tiny sounds he could hear – the electric clock ticking, the fridge drumming faintly, wind in the trees outside.

Sure then, that he was quite alone, he got up, called the dog without looking at it, opened the back door and sent it tottering out into the night. He shut and locked the door, turned back into the kitchen and with a fumbling hand began searching for the key to his old room. When he found it, he grabbed it like a prisoner might the key to his cell.

Climbing the stairs left him so out of breath that, reaching the coconut matting, he had to sit down, resting his head in his hands. Nearly there! But he was dizzy. The threads in the matting zigzagged, disappeared. He shut his eyes, afraid now that his body had deposited him there, no more than a few paces from the room. He fancied that, finding him there, Mrs Moore would have sniffed with disgust, bundled his body away rolled in the matting, so as not to have to touch it. 'Bury this!' she'd have ordered, thinking, that's where it belongs – outside. It never should have been given house room! No. Muddles again. Obscene muddling. And light was coming back, anyway. The threads were still.

Holding on to the wall, Sadler got up, brought his head up slowly and looked around him. His hand was clutching the key so tightly that it was digging into his palm.

Then he walked to his door, put the key in the lock and felt it turn. The door handle was stiff – always had been, hadn't it? But the door moved, and now there he was. He had only to reach out a hand to put on the light.

Cobwebs touched his arm. As the light came on, he saw a huge spider scurry in sideways panic under the bed, disappear into the darkness that held – must hold! – something that lay stinking there, hiding from him and from the light, but God Jesus making such a stench that he wanted to turn and run.

Sadler stood and stared at his room. The walls were yellowed, stained ochre, the damp pushing out wet fungus where the eaves met them. The bed, brass black, its filthy mattress half eaten away, was all that the room contained. The window, grey-curtained by spiders, had been robbed even of its wooden rail that had held once some patterned fabric, too short for the window, but offering a garden for his eyes to wander in – urns, wasn't it, and roses on a grey-green sky? No sign of a rag, even, that might have been those curtains, and there, on the wall above the bed where the picture should have been, a space, just a square of wallpaper paler than the rest.

Sadler knew he should have turned away. But he had to find the picture – only that – and it occurred to him that it might just be there, in that space under the bed. Because it could have fallen off the wall, and even if the glass were broken and the thing faded to shadows, he might find something in it, surely, that he could bear to look at.

He shuffled forward through the dirt, knelt down, brought his head down till his cheek was almost resting on the floor, and slowly his eyes began to search the space. Something bulky lay in the dirt, completely still and yet moving itself, caressed over and over by white maggot fingers. The body of a rat. There was nothing else there, only more of the dirt and droppings that covered the whole floor. But then, yes. He could see something – under one of the bed legs, a wedge of sorts, a piece of paper, was it, folded? Sadler stretched out his hand and tugged it free. He knelt up and shook the dirt from it, unfolded a once bright little picture of sailboats on blue water. It was a card. 'To wish you well' it said, and underneath, in Annie Sadler's writing, 'Happy Birthday, Jack'.

That was it, then. His old room, the little central cell around which his life had arranged itself, he had let die.

Holding his nose, he got up, turned, slammed the door shut and locked it and limped as quickly as he could down the back stairs. He went into the kitchen, opened the back door and began calling to the dog. Tomorrow, he thought, he would have to give it a name.

ROSE TREMAIN

THE CUPBOARD

When Erica March composes herself to die in a cupboard she knows that Ralph Pears will find her. For at the age of 87, she has told the young journalist the richly coloured story of her life as novelist, political activist and, above all, lover, from childhood in Suffolk, Paris between the wars, to oblivion in postwar London. At the end of Ralph's patient probings only one secret remains: the mystery inside the one constant object in her life – her cupboard.

'Much of the power of the book springs from Erica herself, a magnificent and greatly sympathetic creation . . . Miss Tremain has fashioned the totality of one life – and conveyed the evanescence of all human existence'
Janice Elliott in The Sunday Telegraph

'Deeply evocative . . . a book brimming with life – remarkable'
Nicholas Shakespeare in The Times

'Strongly constructed . . . highly relevant . . . thoroughly fascinating'
Richard Brown in The Sunday Times

'Rose Tremain has managed to get into the skin of her clever and wilful old heroine'
Nina Bawden in The Daily Telegraph

sceptre

ROSE TREMAIN

LETTER TO SISTER BENEDICTA

Fat and fifty, educated only to be a wife and mother, Ruby Constad has reached a point of crisis. Her husband, Leon, lies in a nursing home after a stroke that has left him paralysed; her grown-up children are gone. In her anguish Ruby appeals for help to a half-remembered figure from her colonial Indian girlhood – Sister Benedicta. Gradually, the events leading up to Leon's stroke are revealed and a woman emerges whose capacity to love, hope and understand are far greater than she realizes.

'Miss Tremain does something to restore my confidence in the vitality of the English novel . . . LETTER TO SISTER BENEDICTA should be seen as a triumph of the human spirit over the afflictions which beset us. Funny, sad and intensely moving, it is a joy to read from beginning to end'
Auberon Waugh

'The fact that Ruby Constad emerges so strong and devoid of self-pity makes her one of the most generous and complete of modern heroines'
Caroline Moorehead in The Times

'An original talent clears the hurdle of a second novel with pathos and humour'
Christopher Wordsworth in The Guardian

NATALYA LOWNDES

ANGEL IN THE SUN

'The time is 1917–18, the place is a vast estate in south-east Russia . . . The reckless goings-on in the Great House are an echo of the collapse of order and authority outside . . . The peasants are in a state of violent mutiny, a faction of the Red Army is approaching . . . Natalya Lowndes has a passion for the country's savage history, as urgent as a physical sense . . . She is a powerful writer'

Penelope Fitzgerald

'Natalya Lowndes has written a haunting novel, showing an isolated civilisation in miniature fighting for survival . . . Lowndes is a name for the '90s'

She

'A feast of a book, marvellously written, and with an authentic Russian vastness and prolixity . . . the underlying structure is quite wonderful. Threads which appear to have been spun at random are skilfully picked up, and woven into a breathtaking whole, as unforgettable as a vivid dream. Natalya Lowndes has turned a historical footnote into splendid and original fiction'

The Sunday Times

sceptre

RONALD FRAME

PENELOPE'S HAT

Hats had always mattered to novelist Penelope Milne: to project an image; to mark a change of direction or capture a mood; to disguise. In all shapes and materials they punctuate the intriguing story of her life and loves, a tale rich in incident, strange coincidences and sudden deaths. Like the enigmatic Penelope though, her fictional biography is not all it seems. With subtle humour, Ronald Frame blurs the borders between fact and fiction, art and artifice in this many-layered, unforgettable novel.

'Sinuously clever'
The Sunday Times

'A very readable narrative by a considerable talent'
Evening Standard

'A dazzling, diverting read'
The Daily Telegraph

'Fascinating in a subtly observed way'
New Woman

'Frame has a conjuror's dexterity and a real gift for invention which make him a marvellous storyteller'
Literary Review

sceptre

Current and forthcoming titles from Sceptre

LYNDALL P. HOPKINSON

**NOTHING TO FORGIVE: A DAUGHTER'S
LIFE OF ANTONIA WHITE**

RICHARD RUSSO

THE RISK POOL

LISA ST AUBIN DE TERAN

**OFF THE RAILS:
MEMOIRS OF A TRAIN ADDICT**

JANICE ELLIOTT

LIFE ON THE NILE

WILLIAM McILVANNEY

WALKING WOUNDED

BOOKS OF DISTINCTION